THE CURVE THAT CHANGED EVERYTHING

Overcoming Back Pain, Reclaiming Life,
and Moving Beyond Fear—*Without Surgery*

Because healing isn't a straight line—it's a curve

Dr. Yashwant Peddenti (PT)

 Scribe

The Curve That Changed Everything

Publisher: Inkscribe Publishing Pvt. Ltd.

ISBN Number: 978-1-966421-89-4

For every soul who has stumbled but kept going. For those who faced hardship and still chose to rise, to move, and to believe. This book carries your courage on every page.

CONTENTS

ACKNOWLEDGMENTS

No journey is ever truly solitary, and this book is no exception. It would not have been possible without the love, support, and belief of many remarkable people.

To my family—especially my mother—thank you for your unwavering faith and for being the steady hand behind every step I take.

To my team at The Flexion, who embody the mission of helping people move beyond pain with compassion and dedication—I am endlessly grateful to work alongside you.

To the friends who encouraged me to write this book when it was nothing more than an idea scribbled in my head—thank you for pushing me to bring it to life.

To my patients—every single one of you—thank you for trusting me with your stories. You have been my greatest teachers.

And to myself—for choosing to rise, to write, and to believe.

Finally, to you, the reader: thank you for picking up this book. I hope it brings you not just knowledge, but comfort, courage, and the confidence to move forward.

PROLOGUE

The Day I Lost to a Soap Bar

It wasn't a heroic injury.

There was no epic fall. No high-speed chase. No daring rescue. I was in my bathroom, minding my own business, when a slippery bar of soap skidded out of my hands. I bent down to pick it up—and somewhere between the floor and the sink, my back decided, "Nope. Not today."

A sharp, breath-snatching, panic-inducing pain shot through my spine. There I was, frozen halfway between standing and squatting, negotiating with gravity, dignity, and sheer survival instincts. The soap won. My back lost.

That ridiculous moment taught me something I've witnessed play out time and again—not just in my own body, but in the lives of the hundreds of patients I've treated. Most back pain doesn't begin with a dramatic incident. It sneaks in quietly: a twist, a sneeze, a lift, a yawn. And suddenly, life grinds to a halt.

What breaks people isn't just the pain—it's the fear that follows. "What happened to me? Will I ever move the same way again? Will I need surgery?"

For years, I've answered those questions—one patient, one story, one cautious step at a time. People from every walk of life—CEOs, athletes, teachers, new mothers, grandparents—were each brought to a standstill by back pain that seemed to arrive out of nowhere. Each one not just seeking relief, but yearning for hope.

That's why I do what I do. And that's why I wrote this book.

Some of the individuals you'll meet here even underwent surgery before finding their way to true recovery. But their transformation didn't come from procedures or quick fixes. It came from something far more powerful: movement, knowledge, and the quiet return of confidence in their own bodies.

HOW I BECAME THE PHYSIOTHERAPIST WHO LISTENS TO BACKS

I didn't grow up dreaming of becoming a physiotherapist. In fact, I barely understood what physiotherapy really was until I was knee-deep in my studies. Like most people, I thought it was about sprains, sports injuries, and a handful of stretches. I didn't realize it was about lives. About dignity. About the profound, often overlooked ability to sit, stand, walk, work, or hold a grandchild without pain.

Everything changed when I met real patients. People with real stories. People who weren't just complaining about discomfort—they were quietly battling something that touched every part of their existence. I still remember one of my first patients: a middle-aged man who didn't just carry back pain—he carried fear. Fear of movement. Fear of losing his independence. Fear that the life he once knew was slipping away.

That man didn't need complex explanations or a lecture in biomechanics. He needed someone to say, "I hear you. I see you. And I believe you can get better."

THAT'S WHEN IT CLICKED:

Physiotherapy isn't just about joints, discs, or muscles. It's about people. It's about stories. It's about helping people reclaim their lives.

I chose this path, but in truth, it was my patients who shaped me. Their resilience, their honesty, and their quiet courage taught me what really matters—and they continue to inspire me every single day.

I believe you deserve to understand your body. To stop fearing it. To stop surrendering your life to scans, labels, or outdated beliefs.

Your back isn't broken. Your life is still in motion. Your curve—both the one in your spine and the one in your story—can change.

Let's begin.

It can start today.

A LETTER TO MY PATIENTS (PAST, PRESENT & FUTURE)

Dear Patient,

Whether you're holding this book because of your own back pain or someone you love is going through it, I want to say this: I see you. I hear you. And more importantly—I believe in your ability to heal.

Pain has a way of making people feel isolated. It tells you that you're broken, that your life will never return to what it once was. But here's the truth I've learned from both personal experience and from the hundreds of people I've had the privilege to work with: pain is not the end of your story. It's a chapter—but it's not the whole book.

This book is for you. For the part of you that still hopes, even when it's hard. For the part of you that wants to move, to laugh, to live fully again.

I've written these pages not as an expert above you, but as a guide beside you. And I hope each chapter leaves you a little stronger—not just in body, but in spirit.

With respect and hope,

Dr. Yashwant Peddenti (PT)

HOW TO READ THIS BOOK

This isn't a textbook. It's not a technical manual. It's a conversation.

You don't have to read it cover to cover in one sitting. You can jump into the stories that speak to you most. Some chapters may make you pause and reflect. Others might give you a much-needed laugh or an "aha" moment.

All I ask is this: read with an open mind. Even the smallest shift in thinking can spark a new direction in healing.

There's no test at the end. No perfect way to do this. There's only your journey.

You Might Relate If...

You might relate if you:

Have ever been told your back is damaged beyond repair.

Have ever felt scared to move.

Have found yourself trapped between fear and frustration.

Have been promised magical fixes that didn't work.

Have silently wished for someone to just listen and understand.

If any of this sounds like you, this book was written with you in mind.

WHY I WROTE THIS BOOK

I wrote this book because I saw too many people being let down. I saw people sidelined by fear, by misinformation, by the weight of being told that their body was fragile or broken.

I wanted to change that. I wanted to offer not just knowledge, but hope. To remind people that their spine isn't their enemy. That pain doesn't have to write the final chapter.

Most importantly, I wrote this book because I believe people deserve to feel strong, capable, and alive in their own bodies again.

Let's begin.

THE FORGOTTEN BACKBONE

In the grand design of the human body, the spine is the unsung hero. It carries us through every twist, every step, every breath. Yet, most people never think about their back—until it hurts.

We pamper our skin, our hair, our teeth. But our spine? We forget it, until it forgets us.

This section is an invitation to remember the backbone you were born with—the one that has silently supported every moment of your life. It's time to give it the attention it deserves.

MODERN LIFE IS A SPINE'S WORST ENEMY

Our ancestors moved. They squatted, climbed, stretched, and ran. They didn't sit for hours in front of screens, slouched on couches, or scroll endlessly through devices.

Modern life has tamed our bodies but stressed our spines. We live in the comfort of chairs and conveniences while our backs slowly bear the brunt of this motionless life.

This isn't about guilt. It's about awareness. Movement isn't optional for the spine—it's survival.

7 SPINE LIES WE ALL BELIEVE

❖ Lie #1: "Pain means something is broken."

❖ Lie #2: "Rest is the best medicine for back pain."

❖ Lie #3: "Scans tell the whole story."

❖ Lie #4: "I'll never recover without surgery."

❖ Lie #5: "Once damaged, always damaged."

❖ Lie #6: "Getting older means living in pain."

❖ Lie #7: "My back is fragile."

These are not just misconceptions—they are mental cages that hold people back from healing. Every chapter that follows will gently challenge these lies and replace them with truth, science, and hope.

THE FLEXION WAY: MOVEMENT AS MEDICINE

At The Flexion, we believe movement isn't just exercise—it's life. We believe in education, empowerment, and evidence. We believe that healing begins when fear ends.

The Flexion Way is simple: We help people move beyond pain by helping them move—literally and mentally. Movement is not just what we prescribe—it's who we are.

A Spine Story We All Share

Back pain doesn't discriminate. It finds the young and the old, the athletic and the sedentary, the rich and the poor. It humbles everyone equally.

But here's what I've learned: behind every pain story is a resilience story waiting to be written. You're not just a patient with a problem—you're a person with possibilities.

Let's unlock that story.

ONE

THE MANAGER WHO LOST CONTROL—AND FOUND IT IN MOVEMENT

Rajeev never imagined that something as ordinary as bending to tie his shoelace could change his life. It wasn't a dramatic fall or a heavy lift—just a quiet, forgettable moment that ended with a sharp jolt of pain in his lower back.

"I felt like my body betrayed me," he told me during our first session at The Flexion. I've heard this before—the bewilderment, the disbelief. Different faces, different lives, but the same quiet fear beneath the words.

Rajeev, 42, was an IT manager. His life revolved around long hours at a desk, back-to-back meetings, and the slow erosion of movement. Exercise? Rare. Self-care? Neglected. Like many, he believed back pain was something that happened to other people—until it happened to him.

The pain arrived unannounced. Sitting, standing, lying down—everything became uncomfortable. More than the physical discomfort, it was the uncertainty that consumed him. What was happening? Would he ever feel normal again?

His scan showed a mild disc bulge—nothing severe, nothing surgical. But Rajeev wasn't trapped by his spine. He was trapped by fear and the story he told himself about his body.

The Downward Spiral

I could see it in his eyes: hesitation, frustration, dread. He had stopped walking in the park. He avoided lifting his young son. Even simple tasks felt loaded with threat. Every small twinge became a warning siren in his mind.

I gently explained that pain doesn't always equal harm. Sometimes the body's alarm system becomes too sensitive, sounding off even when there's no real danger. Movement wasn't his enemy—it was his way out.

We didn't rush. We didn't chase perfection. We started small: gentle stretches, short walks, breathing exercises. Each tiny step was a quiet act of rebellion against the fear that had taken hold.

The Return of Confidence

Recovery didn't happen overnight. But gradually, Rajeev began to reclaim pieces of his life. He sat longer at work without dread. He lifted his son without panic. He smiled more, laughed more.

One day, during a session, he grinned and said, "I think I'm finally back to myself."

We both laughed. Not because everything was perfect, but because he was no longer controlled by fear. He wasn't "fixed"—he was free.

The Curve

Rajeev's story is far from rare. So many lose confidence in their bodies—not because of what a scan shows, but because of the meaning they attach to pain.

But the spine is strong. The mind is adaptable. Movement brings freedom.

And just like every curve in life, your story is still unfolding—with strength, with hope, and with possibility.

Still on the Journey

I've met so many people like Ramesh over the years—people who remind me why I do what I do. He was 38, a construction worker whose life revolved around heavy lifting, long hours, and the kind of quiet endurance most of us take for granted. His body was his livelihood—until the day it wasn't.

When he first walked into The Flexion, I could see the weight he carried—not just the physical discomfort, but the fear, the frustration, the way pain had pressed pause on his life. He didn't need to say much. The furrowed brow, the careful steps, the way he cradled his movements told me more than words ever could.

"Doctor, I can't do anything," he said, his voice soft but heavy. "I can't sit. I can't sleep. I can't work. My life is stuck."

It wasn't just his back that was hurting. It was his identity, his confidence, his very sense of self. For someone whose world was built on physical labor, the sudden loss of ability cut deeper than any scan could show.

His MRI revealed a mild disc bulge. Nothing dramatic. Nothing surgical. But I've learned that scans rarely tell the full story. The real pain lives in the mind, in the stories we tell ourselves when life takes a sharp turn.

We started small. Breathing. Stretching. Gentle movements. Every little win—a longer walk, an easier bend—chipped away at the fear that had crept in. He told me stories about work, about how much he missed being useful, about how helpless he felt. And sometimes, we laughed too. Like when he tried a simple stretch and joked, "I feel like an old man learning to dance."

Recovery wasn't a straight line. It rarely is. Some days the pain came back. Some days the doubt came back. But each time, we kept moving. Each time, we reminded the mind—and the body—that it was safe to move forward.

Ramesh didn't have a movie-moment recovery. Most people don't. But he made it back—to work, to life, to himself. The day he came in and told me, grinning, "I carried a bag of cement last week. It wasn't easy, but I did it," I knew the real victory wasn't just in the lifting. It was in the believing.

Not every journey is smooth. Some recoveries are messy, incomplete, and ongoing. But that's okay. The goal is never perfection—it's progress. It's rewriting the story fear tried to tell.

And Ramesh? He's still on the journey. Like all of us.

TWO

DRIVEN TO PAIN, STEERED TO FREEDOM

Vikram was one of those patients whose story stayed with me long after the sessions ended. A 45-year-old cab driver, his life played out behind the wheel—hours of sitting, navigating chaotic traffic, skipping meals, and rarely listening to the quiet whispers his body tried to send him.

When he first walked into The Flexion, I could see that exhaustion had settled into his bones. He wasn't just carrying back pain; he was carrying the weight of survival, of responsibilities, of life on the move with no brakes.

"Doctor," he said, almost with a forced smile, "my back's been shouting for a while now. But I kept telling it to wait. Now I can't even sit through my shifts."

The pain had caught up. It usually does. He was stuck—not just in his seat, but in his mind. He believed his spine had failed him, that his work was over, that his body was beyond repair.

Vikram's scan showed what so many do—a mild disc bulge, some wear and tear. Nothing urgent, nothing surgical. But the real problem wasn't on the scan. It was in the story he had begun to believe: that he was broken, fragile, destined for decline.

I sat with him. I always do. Because before any exercise, before any advice, people need to be seen. I told him what I've told so many: "Your scan doesn't tell the full story. Your spine is stronger than you think. We're not here to chase perfection. We're here to get your life back."

We started slow. Breathing. Gentle movement. Short, manageable walks. It wasn't easy. Some days he doubted everything—his progress, his body, even me. But we kept going.

The Turning Point

One day, something shifted. It wasn't a big dramatic breakthrough—those rarely happen outside of movies. But it was real. He came in and said, "I drove for five hours yesterday. I had to stop twice for stretches, but I did it. I wasn't scared."

That mattered more than any perfect scan ever could.

By the time we wrapped up, Vikram wasn't just moving better—he was living better. He laughed more. He carried himself differently. He still had the occasional flare-up, but it didn't own him anymore.

Recovery wasn't about erasing every trace of pain. It was about handing him back the steering wheel.

The Curve

We're all navigating something. Some roadblocks are physical, some emotional. Sometimes the hardest thing isn't the pain itself—it's the story pain convinces us to believe.

But no matter how far off course we feel, there's always a way forward. Sometimes all it takes is one small turn—a new curve—to change everything.

THREE

THE WOMAN WHO
CHOSE BOTH

Fariha was fifty-four, the kind of woman whose hands carried the history of a family. A devout mother of three, she had spent most of her life between the quiet rhythm of her home, her faith, and her small embroidery business in the old lanes of Hyderabad. But when she arrived at The Flexion, she didn't bring her usual grace. She brought discomfort, worry, and a deep longing for something she feared she was losing: her ability to bow down in prayer without wincing.

"It started during Ramadan last year," she told me gently. "The long standing, the bending—it all became too much. I thought it would pass." She paused, her voice barely above a whisper. "Now even the thought of Tarawih makes me anxious."

Fariha's pain wasn't just physical. It was woven into her spiritual life. The simple act of standing, bowing, and rising—movements that had once felt like breathing—had become foreign, laced with apprehension. She wasn't afraid of the pain itself as much as she was afraid of what it symbolized: a life slowly shrinking.

Her MRI was revealing. Unlike many patients I see, Fariha's scan did show notable disc degeneration at L4-L5, with some nerve root irritation. It matched her symptoms—pain radiating into her right leg, numbness after long standing, and discomfort with forward bending. The findings were real, but they weren't the full story. What mattered more was how her body—and her mind—had responded to those changes

"I'm not here to tell you to stop praying," I reassured her. "We just need to help your body move through it differently. You can have both: your prayer and your peace."

We began gently. Her first session didn't involve exercises—it involved conversation. About her daily rituals, the expectations placed upon her, and the silent guilt she felt for even needing help. It wasn't long before she admitted, "I feel like I'm failing—both as a woman and as a believer."

I shook my head softly. "Your faith isn't measured by how low you can bend. It's in the choice to keep showing up, in whatever form that takes."

Our early work focused on mobility she could trust. We used simple hip openers, gentle lumbar rotations, and easy diaphragmatic breathing—not as exercises to "fix" her but as invitations to reconnect with movement safely. On the plinth, I guided her through small pelvic tilts while seated on a Swiss ball, a smile flickering when she realized how much control she still had.

Her face lit up when I introduced supported half-standing prayers using a wall for balance. "I can still do this," she murmured, a quiet confidence returning.

In the following weeks, we layered in subtle core engagement techniques using lightweight resistance bands and standing glute activation. I taught her how to pace herself during Tarawih by alternating between full prostration and seated prayer—a compromise that allowed both body and spirit to coexist.

We also introduced basic nerve mobility drills—gentle sliders for her sciatic system that gradually eased her leg discomfort. She practiced at home, sometimes with her eldest daughter guiding her through the sequences.

What I loved most was how her language began to change. The words "afraid" and "can't" faded. In their place came "trying" and "learning."

One day, she arrived smiling, a sparkle in her eyes. "I prayed last night without fear," she said quietly. "I rested when I needed to. I felt... capable."

That was the turning point—not the absence of discomfort, but the return of ownership.

Fariha's journey wasn't linear. There were good days and not-so-good ones. But her resilience never wavered. Together, we blended her faith with her physiology, crafting a way of moving that honored both.

In our final session, she said something I won't forget: "I used to think healing meant going back to who I was. Now I see it's about becoming someone new—with both faith and flexibility."

The Curve

Healing doesn't always mean returning to the past. Sometimes it means rewriting the present— with gentleness, with wisdom, and with the quiet strength to keep moving forward, one step, one breath, one prayer at a time.

FOUR

THE BRIDE WHO CHOSE STRENGTH OVER SUPERSTITION

Priya walked into The Flexion with the kind of heaviness I've come to recognize—not just physical, but emotional. She was twenty-eight, soon to be married, and instead of glowing with excitement, she looked weighed down by fear and frustration.

Her back pain had started innocently enough: a little ache after house chores, stiffness after long drives. But it didn't stop. It grew—slowly at first, then suddenly—and before she knew it, it was dictating her every move.

Her parents had taken her to every possible option: family doctors, Ayurvedic oils, traditional bone-setters, even a priest. Everyone had an opinion. Some told her not to bend. Others told her not to sit. Some warned her to sleep on the floor. A few even whispered superstitions about how maybe this was "bad luck" before the wedding.

"I just want to walk down the aisle without limping or holding my back," she told me in our first session. There was a crack in her voice, the sound of someone who had tried everything and found nothing.

Her scan showed what so many do—minor disc changes, mild degeneration. But I knew immediately that the pain wasn't just in her spine. It was in her mind: the weight of every bad suggestion, every fearful look, every layer of unnecessary restriction that had wrapped itself around her life.

We started by talking. By understanding. By untangling the fear that had built up. I told her what I tell so many: "Your spine is strong. Your body knows how to heal. We just have to help it remember."

The exercises were gentle at first. Simple movements, breathing, small steps. But with each passing week, Priya grew not just stronger—but braver.

She told me about the wedding shopping she was missing. About the sari fittings she couldn't attend because standing too long made her anxious. About the relatives who told her she was 'too fragile' to carry gifts, to dance, to laugh.

We worked through it—slowly, steadily. We laughed, too. Like the time she tried a simple stretch and said, "If I'm not careful, I'll end up in my wedding album sitting in a chair the whole time."

By the final few sessions, Priya was standing taller. She walked into the clinic one afternoon glowing—not because the pain had vanished entirely, but because the fear had.

"I'm ready," she said. "I'm not scared anymore. I'm going to walk into that wedding and I'm going to dance, even if it's just a little."

I smiled because I knew she would. And she did.

The Curve

Pain isn't always about the body. Sometimes it's about the weight of voices, of expectations, of stories that tell us we're weak or broken.

Priya's journey wasn't just about her back. It was about choosing strength over superstition, hope over fear.

And sometimes, that is the most beautiful kind of strength there is.

FIVE

THE SKEPTIC WHO FINALLY STRETCHED HIS MIND

Imran walked into The Flexion the way many skeptics do—shoulders slightly tense, eyes scanning the room, wearing an expression that said, "Let's get this over with."

"I'm only here because my wife forced me," he announced within minutes, half-grinning. "To be honest, I don't believe this physiotherapy stuff works. But she made me promise I'd give it a shot."

I smiled. I've seen this before. The reluctant husband. The man who's tried every pill, every painkiller, every home remedy handed over like a court summons by well-meaning friends and family. By the time they walk into my clinic, they aren't just battling back pain—they're battling disappointment.

Imran was 36, a software engineer by profession, and his backache had been his shadow for years. Sitting long hours, working late into the night, and ignoring the early whispers of discomfort—until the whispers grew into a roar.

His scan, like so many I've seen, showed mild disc changes. Nothing surgical. Nothing dramatic. Yet his life had changed completely. He avoided long car rides, refused to join friends on weekend getaways, and had practically given up playing with his niece.

We began where I always do—with conversation. I let him tell me everything: the countless doctors, the scan reports, the pain that became his new normal. And then I told him what I tell every patient: "Your scan doesn't define you. Pain doesn't mean damage. And most importantly, this doesn't have to be permanent."

The exercises were simple—embarrassingly simple, in his words. Breathing drills, gentle stretches, short walks. He raised his eyebrows more than once. But he kept showing up.

Week after week, Imran returned. Sometimes with skepticism, sometimes with sarcasm, but he returned. Gradually, I saw the shift—not just in his body, but in his eyes.

He told me about how he once googled every possible spine condition at 2 AM. About how he had a drawer full of blister packs from pharmacies he couldn't even name. About how he hated how small his world had become.

The Turning Point

Then, one day, something changed. He walked in smiling. "I drove to the outskirts last weekend," he said. "Two hours. Stopped once for stretches. But I did it. And I wasn't scared."

That's the real win—the shift from fear to freedom. His back wasn't magically healed overnight. But his life was his again.

The Curve

Imran's story reminds me every day: skepticism is human. Fear is human. But neither one is permanent.

Sometimes the biggest stretch isn't in the muscles—it's in the mind. And when the mind stretches, everything else follows.

SIX

THE INFLUENCER WHO HAD TO UNLEARN EVERYTHING

Tanvi was one of those people who lit up the room the moment she stepped in. But I could tell from the way she held herself that something wasn't right. She was in her late twenties, a fitness and wellness influencer with over two million followers on social media—known for her yoga flows, handstands, and mobility reels that made everything look effortless.

Except that day, nothing was effortless.

She limped slightly as she entered The Flexion, wearing oversized sunglasses and a polite smile that didn't quite reach her eyes. "I think I pulled something," she said casually, "probably just overdid it on one of my videos. It's nothing serious."

But the way she moved told a different story.

We sat down, and I listened as she explained. She'd been filming when her back locked up mid-pose. Since then, any movement—sitting, standing, bending—had become uncomfortable. But what worried her most wasn't just the pain. It was how to keep up the illusion online while silently dealing with the fallout.

"I can't let people know I'm injured," she said softly. "I'm the one who's supposed to help others stay active."

Her scan, like so many, showed mild disc irritation. Nothing dramatic. Nothing irreversible. But her mind had spiraled—what if she couldn't move like before? What if people stopped following her? What if she lost herself?

I told her gently, "Tanvi, you're not your content. And your body isn't broken. Sometimes, healing isn't about pushing harder—it's about listening differently."

We started with the basics. Diaphragmatic breathing. Awareness. Movements stripped of glamour and showmanship. She joked once, "If my followers could see me now, they'd unfollow me instantly." We both laughed because there was truth in it.

The hardest part wasn't the stretches—it was the unlearning. Letting go of the pressure to perform, to be perfect, to chase the next viral move. Slowly, she began to understand that real strength isn't always visible. Sometimes it's quiet, patient, and messy.

The Shift

One day, weeks into therapy, she told me: "I posted a reel yesterday—just me walking outdoors. Nothing fancy. And people actually loved it."

That's when I knew we'd turned the corner. Her body was improving, yes—but her mindset had shifted too.

The Curve

We live in a world that celebrates highlights, not healing. But sometimes, the most important stories are the ones we don't post—the ones where we slow down, breathe, and begin again.

Tanvi reminded me: it's okay to unlearn. To choose real over perfect. And to remember that we're all more than what we show the world.

When Money Isn't the Answer

Arvind walked into The Flexion looking exactly like the man he was—a successful businessman, sharply dressed, every detail polished to perfection. But despite all that control, all that confidence, his eyes gave him away.

He was in pain. And he was frustrated.

"Doctor," he said, almost like he was making a business pitch, "I've seen the best doctors, bought the best chairs, even tried some alternative stuff. Nothing has worked. I need to fix this fast."

I've met many like Arvind over the years—people who are used to solving problems with speed, resources, and sheer willpower. But pain doesn't play by those rules.

We sat down, and I listened. Not just to his words, but to everything unsaid. The weariness. The helplessness. The disbelief that something as simple—and as human—as back pain could bring him to his knees when nothing else in life had.

I told him gently, "Some things can't be rushed. And some answers don't come from doing more, buying more, or searching harder. Sometimes healing begins with less."

We started small. Gentle breathing. Basic movement. The kind of progress that doesn't come with fanfare. At first, he looked almost amused. But he showed up. Again and again.

Slowly, his perspective shifted. He stopped asking how fast he'd recover and started noticing the little things: sitting more comfortably, walking without fear, sleeping without constant discomfort.

The Curve Continues

Some lessons can't be bought.Some journeys can't be rushed.Some stories aren't about endings at all—They're about learning to walk the winding path with grace, patience, and quiet strength.

Pause & Reflect

Think back to a time when your body surprised you—

when you did something you once believed was beyond you.

What did that moment reveal about your resilience?

SEVEN

THE POSTMAN WHO
KEPT WALKING

Raghavan was seventy-two, a man whose life had been defined by motion. For nearly forty years, he had delivered letters through the winding streets of Secunderabad, his steady walk as dependable as the sunrise. He had worn out more shoes than he could remember, but he'd never worn out his sense of purpose. Until now.

When he arrived at The Flexion, his walk had changed. Each step seemed guarded, the right foot reluctant. "The scan shows disc bulges and arthritis," he said softly, folding and unfolding the edge of his handkerchief. "They told me it's my age. I'm afraid I'll have to stop walking altogether."

His MRI painted a familiar picture: multilevel degenerative disc disease, mild canal narrowing, right-sided foraminal stenosis. Enough to explain the discomfort—backache, morning stiffness, occasional numbness—but it wasn't the pain that concerned him most. It was the thought of stopping, of losing the identity built on decades of movement.

"I've always walked," he said with quiet despair. "If I stop, I don't know who I'll be."

Our first step wasn't exercise—it was a conversation. I explained that scans, while useful, didn't write the future. We spoke of how the body could adapt, how strength could be rebuilt gently, and how fear often tightens the body more than any physical limitation. He nodded, though doubt still clouded his eyes.

We started small. Seated pelvic tilts on a firm chair, gentle spinal mobility exercises to restore some ease in movement. I taught him diaphragmatic breathing—not the kind used in formal meditation, but simply as a way to release the tension he had unknowingly held for years.

In the following sessions, we added seated marching to strengthen his hip flexors and gentle sit-to-stand repetitions to build leg strength. He smiled quietly when he realized he could do more than he thought. I introduced light Theraband exercises—glute bridges, side-stepping with gentle resistance, and wall-supported mini squats. For balance, we practiced tandem walking near the wall and simple weight shifts on foam pads.

The biggest shift wasn't in his muscles but in his mindset. He told me he had avoided his morning walks for months, fearing a fall. I encouraged him to walk again—short distances at first, with rests as needed, not to chase speed but to restore routine. "It's not about how far," I reminded him, "it's about showing up."

We also addressed the nerve sensitivity that sometimes tingles down his leg. I taught him gentle nerve sliders for the sciatic nerve—small, controlled movements that didn't provoke his symptoms but gradually reduced his discomfort. On days when the heaviness in his back returned, he used a warm compress and a home TENS unit for relief. He began to understand that discomfort didn't mean damage, and pain didn't have to mean panic.

In our fifth session, I brought in gentle step-up exercises using a low platform, progressing gradually to support heel raises and resistance band walks. His balance and coordination, once shaky, began to improve. "I feel steadier," he admitted, surprised. "Like I'm standing taller without even trying."

As the weeks passed, Raghavan's steps grew more confident. He returned to his morning walks, not every day, but enough to feel the old rhythm returning. He shared how he once loved stopping by the small temple on his route, chatting with neighbors, and buying flowers for his wife. Those moments, he said, made him feel alive. Slowly, he began reclaiming them.

One morning, he arrived at the clinic smiling wider than I'd seen before. "I walked to the temple today," he said, his voice carrying both pride and disbelief. "I rested halfway, but I made it. Without fear."

We didn't aim for perfection. His scan still showed wear, but what had changed was his relationship with it—and with his own story. He no longer saw himself as broken, but as someone who could adapt, who could keep moving despite the labels written in radiology reports.

In our final session, as he adjusted his old cap, he said something that stayed with me: "I don't need to walk fast. I don't need to walk far. I just need to know I can still walk."

The Curve

Healing isn't always about erasing the marks life leaves behind. Sometimes it's about learning to carry them differently—with patience, quiet courage, and the steady choice to keep moving forward, one step at a time.

EIGHT

THE ATHLETE WHO SWAPPED SPEED FOR LONGEVITY

Arjun walked into The Flexion like so many athletes I've seen—young, determined, and restless. At just twenty-three, he was already a state-level cricketer with dreams of making it to the national stage. His life revolved around training, practice, and performance. But recently, something had started holding him back.

His back.

"It started as a dull ache after practice," he told me. "But now it's there even when I'm not playing. I can't afford to sit out, Doc. I'll lose my spot."

I've heard this fear before—the fear that slowing down equals failure. For athletes, especially those on the cusp of something big, rest feels like a threat.

But the truth is, the very drive that fuels their ambition can sometimes push their bodies too far.

Arjun's movement told me what I needed to know. Tight hips. Overactive lower back. Glutes barely firing. Classic signs of imbalance from repetitive stress.

We sat down, and I explained what I explain so often: "Pain is your body's way of asking for attention, not punishment. Ignoring it won't make you stronger. Listening to it will."

We started small. Focused breathing. Gentle mobility. Glute activation that made him roll his eyes at first. For someone used to speed and intensity, this slower pace felt foreign. He joked once, "I feel like a ninety-year-old in these sessions."

But he kept showing up. And slowly, the pieces began to shift. His movements grew smoother. His mind calmed. He stopped treating rest as the enemy.

The Outcome

He didn't win the tournament that season. And that was okay. Because what he gained was bigger: the knowledge that his career wasn't a sprint—it was a marathon. He learned that taking care of his body wasn't weakness—it was wisdom.

The Curve

Arjun's story is a reminder that sometimes the hardest race isn't the one on the field—it's the race within. The pressure to push, to prove, to perform.

But slowing down doesn't mean giving up. Sometimes it's the bravest move we make—the one that keeps us in the game for the long run.

"Healing isn't the absence of pain. It's the return of confidence."

NINE

THE GIRL WHO FOUND
HER BALANCE

Aarohi was sixteen when she first came to The Flexion. She walked in quietly, her shoulders slightly hunched, her eyes darting nervously around the room. I could tell immediately she wasn't just carrying physical discomfort—she was carrying the weight of self-consciousness.

Her parents brought her in after a school health check revealed mild scoliosis—an unexpected curve in her spine that left her feeling different, fragile, and more than a little frightened. The word itself—scoliosis—had already begun to shape how she saw herself.

She told me softly, "I keep thinking people will notice. I feel like I'm standing wrong all the time."

I've worked with many young people like Aarohi—bright, thoughtful, and burdened by the sudden realization that their body doesn't quite fit the image they had in mind. Fear isn't always about pain. Sometimes, it's about being seen as "less than," "flawed," or "broken."

We sat together, and I told her what I knew she needed to hear: "Your spine is just one part of you. You're not broken. And we're not here to chase perfection—we're here to help you move with confidence."

We started with breathing exercises and simple mobility—small movements that didn't overwhelm. She was hesitant at first. I could see her second-guessing every motion, worrying about her "curve." But with each session, she began to trust her body again.

Sometimes we laughed—like the time she stumbled during a balance exercise and called herself a "baby giraffe." Little by little, her fear softened. Her movements grew smoother. Her smile returned.

We didn't obsess over straight lines. We celebrated fluidity. We celebrated the play. We celebrated the truth that bodies, like lives, don't have to be symmetrical to be strong.

The Curve

When Aarohi finished her sessions, she stood taller—not because her spine was suddenly flawless, but because her confidence was. She learned that balance isn't about being perfect. It's about moving forward even when things feel uncertain.

And that's a lesson many of us need to carry: sometimes the most beautiful curves in life are the ones that teach us resilience, kindness, and strength.

TEN

THE MENSTRUAL WARRIOR

Sanika was 26 when she first came to The Flexion. Her expression was guarded, her posture tense, as though her own body had become the enemy. "I don't even remember the last time I had a pain-free period," she said, her voice low, almost apologetic. "It just got worse... and then it stayed."

Her back pain had begun the way it often does for many women—tied to her menstrual cycle. But instead of disappearing, the discomfort took root. It grew. Month after month, year after year, it started leaking into the rest of her life. Sitting, standing, walking—all of it carried an edge of discomfort.

She had seen doctors. She had heard it all: "It's normal." "It's just stress." "It'll settle down." But deep down, she knew something wasn't right. And with every dismissive comment, she had started to believe the worst: that maybe she was just weak. Maybe this was her fault.

I sat with her and listened—really listened. Not just to the words, but to the weight beneath them. I told her gently, "Pain isn't a character flaw. It's not a weakness. And you don't have to live like this."

We began with breathwork and gentle pelvic mobility. Movements that helped her reconnect with parts of her body she had learned to distrust. At first, she was hesitant—unsure whether this could work when so many others had failed her.

But each session built something. Not just physical ease, but belief. We laughed too—like the day she managed a movement without flinching and said, "Maybe my body doesn't hate me after all."

Little by little, the layers of tension unraveled. She started to move without fear, to breathe without bracing. She stopped apologizing for her body.

The Outcome

Her pain didn't vanish overnight. It rarely does. But Sanika reclaimed something far more precious: her confidence, her freedom, and her ability to trust her own strength.

The Curve

Pain can make us feel betrayed by our own bodies. It can shrink our world, dim our light, and erode our trust in ourselves.

But healing is not just the easing of discomfort—it's the quiet return of hope, one breath, one step, one brave moment at a time.

ELEVEN

THE MAN WHO CARRIED HIS PAST ON HIS SPINE

Narsimha was sixty-eight, the kind of man whose face bore the marks of resilience: deep lines carved by years of labor, illness, and quiet endurance. He had survived something most people in his neighborhood still whispered about—spinal tuberculosis, or as many still called it, "Pott's Disease."

"I had TB of the spine in my thirties," he told me, his voice soft but steady. "I was in bed for nearly a year back then. They said I would never stand straight again. But I did."

He had, indeed. He returned to work, raised a family, and lived without complaint. But now, decades later, he found himself shrinking back into the fear he thought he had left behind. "My back is stiff," he admitted. "And there's a deep ache when I move. Part of me keeps wondering—what if it comes back?"

His old X-rays showed the typical sequelae of healed spinal TB: fused vertebrae at the thoracolumbar junction, mild kyphosis, and some degenerative changes. There was no active infection. No danger. But his body moved like it still remembered the fear—the way he guarded his spine, the hesitation in his steps, the way he sat stiff-backed as if he might break.

I listened more than I spoke. People like Narsimha didn't just carry physical scars. They carried memories of suffering in an era when medical care was sparse and knowledge scarcer. His biggest hurdle wasn't his back—it was the belief that his spine was permanently fragile.

Our sessions began with education. I explained how the infection was long gone, how the fusion in his spine was stable, and how movement could help, not harm. He nodded cautiously, but I could see the weight of old warnings lingering.

We started gently. Seated thoracic rotations, cat-camel mobility drills, and supported side bends. Movements designed to reassure his nervous system that change was possible without harm. His initial stiffness was more from fear than fused joints.

I introduced diaphragmatic breathing—simple, quiet breathing that softened his protective bracing. Over time, we layered in standing weight shifts, wall-supported squats, and gentle overhead reaches with a lightweight resistance band. Each session brought not just physical ease but the slow unraveling of long-held fear.

One day, while performing a gentle spinal extension over a Swiss ball, he paused and smiled. "I never thought I'd bend backward again," he said, the surprise genuine. "I thought I was locked."

His balance improved. His stride lengthened. He began to carry grocery bags again, and, to his family's amusement, he took morning walks with the neighbors—a ritual he had abandoned years ago.

I also taught him pacing strategies. We used a simple formula: move, rest, move again. This allowed him to gradually build endurance without provoking old aches. He kept a journal, noting down every walk, every small victory. "I feel like I'm getting taller," he chuckled once, patting his back.

In our later sessions, we even introduced light resistance with a therapy band for his upper back, and low-impact cycling to build stamina. Narsimha's fear slowly gave way to quiet confidence.

In our final session, he shared something I'll never forget: "For years, I believed I was broken inside. Now I know I was just… stuck."

The Curve

Healing isn't always about the body alone. Sometimes it's about releasing the weight of old stories—stories that told us we were fragile, that movement was dangerous. It's about rewriting those beliefs with action, with patience, and with the quiet decision to live fully, no matter what the past once said.

TWELEVE

THE MENOPAUSE WARRIOR: A STORY OF STRENGTH BEYOND HORMONES

Shalini was 52 when she came to The Flexion, the kind of woman who carried herself with quiet grace but whose eyes told a different story—one of exhaustion, frustration, and loss. She was a schoolteacher, a mother, a caregiver, and like so many women in her phase of life, she had begun to feel invisible.

Her back pain wasn't the kind that made headlines. It was the dull, persistent ache that crept in gradually, blurring the lines between physical discomfort and emotional fatigue. The kind of pain that wasn't just about muscles or joints—it was woven into her hormones, her identity, her sense of worth.

"I don't even know who I am anymore," she said during our first session. "Everything hurts. I'm always tired. And I feel like I've become... unnecessary."

Her words stayed with me. Pain, especially around menopause, is rarely just physical. It carries the weight of aging, of shifting roles, of years spent putting others first.

We began with small, gentle movements. I guided her through mindful breathing, the kind that calms the nervous system and helps the body feel safe again. It wasn't about flashy exercises—it was about helping her trust her body, one step at a time.

At first, she was hesitant. "This won't work for me," she murmured once. But she kept showing up. And slowly, her posture shifted. Her smile returned. Her world, which had quietly shrunk around her, began to expand again.

The Outcome

Shalini's pain didn't vanish overnight, but her life did change. She rediscovered movement, confidence, and laughter. She stopped apologizing for her age, for her body, for herself.

One day, she told me, half-joking, "I think I'm ready to dance again." And I knew she meant more than just physically.

The Curve

Menopause doesn't mark the end of strength—it marks a new chapter of it. Shalini reminded me that healing isn't always about youth or hormones—it's about resilience, hope, and the quiet decision to keep moving forward, no matter what.

THIRTEEN

BACK IN THE GAME: A RECREATIONAL ATHLETE'S STORY

Rohan arrived at The Flexion with the unmistakable restlessness of someone used to moving fast—only now he couldn't. At 35, he was a recreational runner and football enthusiast whose life, for years, revolved around weekend marathons, evening matches, and early morning jogs. Until the day his back said no.

"It started as a pinch," he told me, frustration etched into every word. "I thought it was nothing. But it kept coming back. Now, even sitting makes me nervous."

I could see what was happening—his body wasn't broken, but his confidence in it was. He'd gone from movement being his escape to it becoming his fear.

We started with simple mobility drills and gentle stability exercises. I avoided calling them 'rehab'—

for someone like Rohan, that word felt too clinical. Instead, I framed it as 'getting back to the game' in small steps.

He was impatient. Of course he was. Athletes—even recreational ones—measure progress in speed, in distance, in time. But this wasn't that kind of race.

Gradually, the shifts came. Subtle, but real. He started to jog short distances. He noticed he could stand longer, sleep better. The constant low-level fear began to dissolve.

We talked a lot about mindset—the danger of defining yourself by performance alone. About finding joy in movement without needing to push limits every time. He laughed when I told him, "Your spine isn't a ticking time bomb. It's just asking for balance."

The Outcome

Eventually, Rohan returned to running. He even played football again. But he did it differently—listening, adapting, respecting his body instead of punishing it.

The Curve

Rohan's story reminded me that sometimes the greatest strength lies not in how fast we can go, but in knowing when to pause, reset, and start again—smarter, calmer, stronger.

FOURTEEN

THE PRIEST WHO BOWED AGAIN

Ramamurthy was sixty-one, a man whose entire life had revolved around rhythm: the ringing of temple bells, the quiet chant of mantras, the daily rituals of bowing, standing, offering, and serving. For over three decades, he had been the chief priest of a small, ancient Shiva temple tucked into the heart of a bustling South Indian town.

When he first arrived at The Flexion, he walked carefully, hands folded over his abdomen, with the reverence of someone stepping onto sacred ground. "My back," he said softly, "It no longer allows me to serve my Lord properly."

The weight of his words was clear. His pain wasn't just physical. It was spiritual. The inability to bow fully in namaskara, to sit cross-legged on the temple floor during rituals, to climb the narrow stairs to the sanctum—these weren't small inconveniences. They were central to his identity.

His MRI revealed moderate degenerative changes: lumbar spondylosis with facet joint hypertrophy, mild disc protrusions, and some foraminal narrowing. Enough to explain discomfort, but not the crippling pain he described. A classic case of scan findings not fully matching the severity of symptoms.

"I've stopped doing the early morning puja," he whispered, his eyes moist. "The body fails. The heart wants to continue.

Our first session wasn't about movement—it was about permission. Permission to acknowledge grief, frustration, and fear. I explained that while his spine showed some age-related changes, there was no evidence of dangerous instability. His pain was real, but it wasn't necessarily permanent.

We began gently. His daily prayers required prolonged standing, forward bends, and kneeling—so we focused on modifying these patterns safely. Seated lumbar mobility with supported forward reaches, supine pelvic tilts, and gentle lower limb nerve glides formed the core of his initial plan.

Ramamurthy was curious by nature. He asked about the science behind each movement. I explained that pain could sometimes linger in the nervous system long after tissues had healed. That our goal was to restore his confidence in motion.

I introduced graded exposure therapy: he practiced partial bowing using a high table for support, progressing slowly towards deeper bends. He learned to transition from standing to kneeling with cushions and hand support, so he could safely participate in temple rituals again.

To improve his tolerance for standing during long prayers, we incorporated calf and hip endurance work using light resistance bands. For his core stability, we used quadruped alternate arm-leg lifts—modified versions to respect his mobility limits.

One technique that made a visible difference was proprioceptive retraining: simple closed-chain weight shifts on soft pads, barefoot when possible, connecting mind and body. This helped reduce his exaggerated muscle guarding.

In parallel, I addressed his breathing. Many of his movements were held tense, breath shallow. I guided him through coordinated breathing patterns with spinal motion—a simple inhale on extension, exhale on flexion—integrating the breath work into his daily routines.

Ramamurthy practiced with dedication. He told me he recited his Gayatri mantra mentally while holding gentle stretches, blending prayer with rehabilitation. This union seemed to soothe him more than any single exercise.

Weeks passed. His movement deepened. His ability to kneel for short durations returned. His confidence in standing longer during evening rituals improved. The pain wasn't entirely gone, but his relationship with it had softened.

One morning, he walked into the clinic with vibhuti on his forehead and a quiet smile. "I did the full abhishekam this morning," he said, eyes glistening. "Not without effort, but without fear."

In our final session, he placed both hands together in namaste. "I used to believe that my devotion depended on my ability to bow. Now I understand—it is the willingness to keep showing up that matters."

The Curve

Healing often asks us to redefine the meaning of devotion—not just to faith, but to the body, to movement, and to the life we wish to continue living. Some days we bow deeply. Some days we bow gently. But every act of movement, however small, is still an offering of hope.

FIFTEEN

THE MOTHER WHO LEARNED TO HOLD HERSELF TOO

Shruti came to The Flexion looking every bit like the new mothers I've seen countless times—tired, tentative, and carrying more than just her newborn. She carried the invisible weight of expectations, exhaustion, and the kind of quiet guilt only new mothers truly understand.

Her back pain had started during her pregnancy but lingered months after delivery. She brushed it off for a while, telling herself it was normal, that it would settle. But it didn't. And now it had started seeping into every part of her day—from feeding her baby to simply standing for too long.

"I feel like my body isn't mine anymore," she confessed, her voice barely above a whisper. "It's like I'm only here to take care of everyone else. I don't even know how to take care of myself."

Her words were ones I'd heard before but never took lightly. Postnatal pain isn't just physical—it's deeply emotional. It's about losing trust in your own body at a time when the world expects you to give more than you've ever given.

We began with small movements. Breath-led mobility. Gentle postural resets. It wasn't about intensity—it was about safety, reassurance, and rediscovering ease in her own skin.

Shruti doubted herself at first. She hesitated with every movement, unsure if she'd make things worse. But she kept showing up. And gradually, something shifted—not just in her spine but in her eyes.

She told me once, smiling softly, "For the first time, I feel like I'm standing tall—not just for my baby, but for myself."

The Outcome

Shruti's pain eased. Her confidence returned. She didn't just heal—she reclaimed herself. The way she held her child changed too—no longer from a place of bracing, but from steadiness.

The Curve

Some of the strongest people I meet are those who give the most of themselves—often without pause. Shruti reminded me that sometimes the greatest strength isn't in holding others—it's in learning to hold ourselves too.

SIXTEEN

THE MAN WHO FINALLY LOOKED DEEPER

Venkatesh was forty-nine when he arrived at The Flexion, his face a mix of resignation and quiet frustration. His back pain had been his unwelcome companion for nearly two years. He had done the rounds: multiple doctors, home remedies, Ayurveda, acupuncture, painkillers, and two physiotherapists before me. Nothing had offered lasting relief.

"I've tried everything," he said softly. "I'm just tired now."

His movements were guarded. He held his lower back constantly, as if afraid it might shatter with the slightest wrong step. Yet despite the relentless pain, he had refused any imaging or diagnostic investigations. "Scans will only show something bad," he murmured. "What's the point?"

This isn't uncommon. Many patients avoid diagnostics out of fear—fear of labels, fear of worst-case scenarios. Others avoid them because they've already been told their pain is "all in their head."

I listened. Carefully. His description was precise: constant low back ache, occasional low-grade fever, night sweats, weight loss he brushed off as stress. He had no significant history of trauma. He was visibly tired—not just physically, but mentally. His case didn't feel like the usual mechanical back pain we see daily.

I gently suggested that imaging wasn't about chasing fear—it was about clarity. About knowing whether we were dealing with something mechanical, inflammatory, infectious, or something else entirely. After some discussion, he agreed to a basic MRI and blood work.

The results were revealing. His MRI showed early signs of infective spondylodiscitis—an infection of the intervertebral disc and adjacent vertebral bodies. Blood markers confirmed mild elevation of inflammatory markers.

It wasn't just "back pain." It was an infection—rare, but real.

When I explained the findings to him, he went silent. "So it wasn't just in my head," he said after a long pause.

"It never was," I assured him.

The next steps involved collaboration. He was referred to an infectious disease specialist for antibiotic management while I outlined a gentle, staged rehabilitation plan. We agreed that recovery would take time—and that the first priority was addressing the infection.

We began movement only after his medical treatment stabilized. I introduced gentle, unloaded exercises: supine pelvic tilts, deep diaphragmatic breathing, and lower limb mobility to prevent deconditioning. We avoided provocative spinal flexion and heavy loading. The goal was to maintain circulation, promote confidence, and prevent stiffness without compromising healing.

Weeks into antibiotic therapy, his fever subsided. His pain reduced gradually, and his sleep improved. As his energy returned, we layered in isometric core activation, bridging variations, and gentle seated rotations. He was cautious but committed.

One session, he looked up and said quietly: "I wish I had done this sooner. The tests, I mean. I kept waiting for the pain to go away on its own."

I nodded. "Sometimes the bravest thing isn't pushing through. It's pausing to understand."

By the third month, Venkatesh was walking longer distances, sleeping through the night, and most importantly—living without the constant mental cloud of undiagnosed pain. We gradually added resistance work with bands, improved his hip mobility, and restored confidence in basic spinal movements.

In our final session, he shared: "I thought getting a scan would bring bad news. But the real bad news was not knowing. I'm glad I finally faced it."

The Curve

Sometimes healing begins not with movement, but with understanding. Pain without clarity can paralyze more than any physical injury. Looking deeper—through knowledge, through testing, through patience—can open the door to hope, even when the path is slow.

SEVENTEEN

THE YOUNG MAN WHO RECLAIMED HIS RHYTHM

Neeraj walked into The Flexion looking more weighed down by worry than by physical discomfort. At just 29, he had recently been diagnosed with Ankylosing Spondylitis—a condition he barely understood but one that had already begun to reshape the way he saw his body, his future, his life.

"I read everything online," he said during our first meeting, anxiety thick in his voice. "It says I'll fuse... that I won't be able to move freely. I'm terrified."

I've met many like him—young, ambitious, blindsided by a diagnosis that feels like a life sentence. The real enemy wasn't just the stiffness or the pain—it was the fear that his life, as he knew it, was slipping away.

We sat. We talked. I reassured him of what I knew to be true: "A diagnosis isn't a destiny. You are not your scan. And your body is capable of far more than you think."

We began with gentle mobility—not overwhelming, not rigid, but fluid and forgiving. I introduced mindful movement practices and strength exercises tailored to his comfort. It wasn't about erasing the diagnosis—it was about giving him agency again.

There were hard days. He'd arrive frustrated, stiff, sometimes angry. But he kept showing up. And gradually, his body followed his mind's quiet decision to hope.

He told me one day, "I danced at my friend's wedding last weekend. Just a little. But I wasn't scared. I felt... normal."

The Outcome

Neeraj didn't just regain physical movement—he reclaimed his rhythm, his joy, his sense of self beyond the weight of a medical label. He learned that even with Ankylosing Spondylitis, life didn't have to stop. It just had to adapt.

The Curve

Sometimes the hardest battle isn't against pain—it's against the stories we believe about our future. Neeraj taught me that even when life throws us the unexpected, we can still choose to move. To dance. To find our rhythm again.

EIGHTEEN

THE MAN WHO STEPPED BACK INTO HIS LIFE

Ramesh came to The Flexion looking like a man quietly weighed down—not just by back pain, but by the shrinking of a life he once loved. At 42, he had been the kind of father who played Sunday cricket, chased his daughter through the park, and laughed without hesitation. But that version of him felt distant, replaced by stiffness, fear, and quiet resignation.

"I don't remember the last time I ran, Doctor," he told me softly. "My daughter asked why I don't come to the park anymore. I didn't know what to tell her."

His words lingered. Because pain doesn't just settle in muscles or joints—it creeps into memories, empties spaces, and slowly rewrites the story of who we are.

We began gently. Seated mobility, easy postural resets, nothing intimidating or overwhelming. No talk of weight, no criticism—just permission to move again, one careful breath, one hopeful shift at a time.

At first, Ramesh moved like he was bracing for something to snap. But with each visit, a quiet transformation began. His steps grew steadier. His face softened. His world, once narrowed by fear, started to expand.

I'll never forget the day he came in glowing:

"I walked to the park," he said. "I didn't run. But I walked. And my daughter held my hand the whole way."

The Outcome

Ramesh didn't chase perfection. He rediscovered the possibility. He learned that recovery isn't always about erasing every discomfort—it's about reclaiming the moments pain tries to steal.

The Curve

The greatest victories often arrive unnoticed: a walk under open skies, a hand held, a step taken not in haste, but in quiet triumph.

Ramesh reminded me: movement isn't just medicine. It's memory, connection, and the quiet return of life itself.

A Moment to Pause

What is one thing you've stopped doing—not because you can't, but because somewhere along the way, you started believing you shouldn't?

What gentle step could bring you back to it—without pressure, without apology, without fear?

NINTEEN

THE WOMAN WHO REFUSED TO DISAPPEAR

Leela came to The Flexion at 73, her eyes carrying the kind of tiredness that doesn't come from age alone. She had suffered a compression fracture months earlier and since then, her world had quietly begun to shrink. Simple things—standing at the window, tending to her plants, stepping outside—had faded from her daily life.

"It's like I'm becoming invisible," she told me softly. "Everyone fusses over me, but I feel... small. Like I'm disappearing."

Her words settled in my chest. Because sometimes pain isn't just about injury—it's about dignity, identity, and the slow erosion of the life you've built.

We started gently. Seated mobility, breath-led posture work, light standing movements. At first, she was cautious—every step felt like an invitation for something to go wrong. But I reminded her: "Strength isn't always about what you lift.

Sometimes it's about standing tall in your own life again."

With each session, Leela's confidence returned. We celebrated the small victories: standing a little longer, walking without clutching the walls, lifting her chin when she moved. And slowly, her laughter returned too.

One day, she arrived beaming: "I watered my plants this morning. First time in months." The pride in her voice said everything.

The Outcome

Leela didn't just regain movement—she reclaimed her presence in the world. She stopped apologizing for her body and started living in it again.

The Curve

Aging doesn't mean disappearing. Leela reminded me that no matter how many years pass, the desire to be seen, to belong, to move with dignity—never fades.

And sometimes, the most courageous thing we can do is simply take the next step.

TWENTY

THE MAN WHO FOUND HIS PACE AGAIN

Ravindra came to The Flexion with the careful steps of a man who no longer trusted his own body. At 68, a retired school principal, he was used to control, routine, and a life of gentle authority. But after a mild stroke and weeks of inactivity, everything about movement now felt foreign.

"It's like my legs forgot who they belong to," he told me in our first session, half-laughing but half-defeated. "Even a short walk feels like a marathon now."

I could hear the frustration behind his words. The real struggle wasn't just physical—it was the slow unraveling of identity. He wasn't battling only weakness. He was battling the quiet belief that his best days were behind him.

We began slowly. Very slowly. Seated posture, breath-focused standing drills, small walking loops. I reminded him gently: "Pace doesn't matter. Presence does. Every step counts, however small."

At first, his movements were stiff, tentative. But he kept coming back. And little by little, something shifted—not just in his legs, but in his expression, his voice, his eyes.

One day, he smiled and said, "I walked to the corner store this morning. Took me time. But I did it. On my own."

The Outcome

Ravindra didn't race back to who he used to be. He didn't have to. He discovered that healing isn't about chasing the past—it's about finding a new rhythm that lets you move forward without fear.

The Curve

Life rarely follows a straight line. Ravindra's story reminded me that progress doesn't always mean speed—it means courage, consistency, and the quiet decision to begin again, no matter how many times we're asked to start over.

TWENTY ONE

THE BOY WHO STEPPED OUTSIDE

Nikhil was 14 when he came to The Flexion, though it was clear from the start that he'd rather have been anywhere else. His parents brought him in after months of slouched posture, neck pain, and complaints of back discomfort. But it wasn't the physical symptoms that worried them most—it was how much he'd withdrawn into himself, tucked away behind screens, gaming consoles, and silence.

He shrugged when I asked him questions, giving me the bare minimum. Until I asked, "What did you used to love doing before this?"

That's when his eyes flickered. "Skateboarding," he mumbled. "I haven't done that in a while."

That was the key.

We didn't start with long lectures or complicated exercises. We started with play—small, playful movements that woke up his curiosity, not just his muscles. Gentle posture resets, balance games, breathing drills disguised as challenges. Slowly, his shell began to crack.

He told me once, grinning, "I tried standing on my board again. Just for a minute. It felt... good."

The Outcome

Nikhil didn't transform overnight. But he stepped outside—both literally and figuratively. He rediscovered movement not as punishment, but as possibility.

The Curve

Sometimes healing isn't about fixing something broken. Sometimes it's about reminding someone who they are beneath the layers of fear, disconnection, or screens.

Nikhil reminded me: no matter how far we drift, there's always a way back—to movement, to joy, to life.

TWENTY TWO

THE BREATH THAT BROUGHT HIM BACK

Arif came to The Flexion carrying something heavier than just physical discomfort. He was in his late thirties, a quiet, soft-spoken man who had recovered from COVID months earlier—but never quite felt like himself again.

"It's like I'm here, but not really," he said, struggling to explain the weariness that lingered in his chest, his back, and somewhere deeper that words couldn't touch. "I can't seem to catch my breath, and my body just... aches."

I've heard this before—the in-between state where you're not sick, but you're far from well. Where the world expects you to move on, but your body hasn't quite caught up.

We started gently. Simple breathing patterns. Subtle mobility. Nothing rushed, nothing forced. I reminded him: "Sometimes the body needs permission to feel safe again before it can move again."

At first, even these basic shifts felt exhausting. But he returned, session after session. We focused on breath—not as exercise, but as reconnection. We added slow stretches, guided movements, the kind that whisper rather than shout.

One day, after weeks of patient work, Arif walked in differently. Taller. Lighter.

"I went for a walk last evening," he told me. "First time in months I didn't feel... fragile."

The Outcome

Arif didn't just reclaim physical stamina. He rediscovered trust—in his breath, his steps, his life.

The Curve

Healing isn't always dramatic. Sometimes it's quiet. It happens breath by breath, in small moments where we realize: we are still here, we are still moving, we are still whole.

Arif reminded me: sometimes the greatest comeback begins not with a leap, but with a single breath.

A Moment to Breathe

When was the last time you allowed yourself to simply stop—

without chasing progress, without proving recovery, without rushing to the next thing?

Sometimes the most powerful way forward begins by standing still,

noticing your breath, and letting life meet you exactly where you are.

TWENTY THREE

STEPS THAT STILL MATTER

Naveen came to The Flexion quietly. He was in his early forties, living with a below-knee prosthetic after an accident years ago. From the outside, he looked like someone who had adapted, moved on, and returned to life. But his eyes told a different story.

"It's not the leg that bothers me," he said during our first session. "It's this constant back ache. I can't seem to shake it off."

I could see the frustration—not just from the discomfort, but from the silent weight of appearing fine while still carrying an invisible burden. Like so many who've faced life-changing injuries, he had grown used to pushing through, not asking for help.

We began gently. Not with exercises, but with conversation. With reassurance that he wasn't imagining things, that his body's compensations were real—and so was his pain.

Gradually, we worked on mobility, postural balance, gentle core activation, and movement strategies that honored both sides of his body. I reminded him: "Every step counts—not because it's perfect, but because it's yours."

He smiled one day, telling me, "I walked to the tea stall near my house without even thinking about it. First time in months."

The Outcome

Naveen's pain eased, but more importantly, he stopped measuring his life by what was lost. He began to move not just with his body—but with his heart back in it too.

The Curve

We all carry visible and invisible scars. Naveen reminded me that healing isn't always about fixing—it's about honoring the steps we can still take, no matter how uneven the path.

TWENTY FOUR

THE GIRL ON WHEELS

Jessica was twenty-four when her life split into before and after.

A road accident had left her with an incomplete spinal cord injury at the thoracic level. In the blink of an eye, the world she knew—the one filled with college friends, early career dreams, laughter, and late-night street food—collapsed into a hospital bed, followed by the confines of a wheelchair.

When she first came to The Flexion, she barely spoke. Her parents pushed her chair in while she kept her head low, arms crossed tightly over her lap. The physical damage was clear—lower limb weakness, poor trunk control, spasms—but the deeper wounds lay unseen.

"I used to be everywhere," she whispered during our first session, eyes brimming but refusing to spill. "Now I'm invisible."

The scans showed incomplete cord damage—there was potential. But potential is a difficult thing when you're twenty-four and the world is already racing ahead without you. She had been told, repeatedly, what she couldn't do. No one had focused on what she still could.

Her daily challenges were endless. Navigating tiny doorways. Facing stares at temples and markets. Listening to neighbors speculate on whether any boy would marry her now. Every act of daily life—brushing her hair, using the bathroom, moving from bed to chair—was a battlefield. She wasn't just fighting her own body. She was fighting how the world saw her.

And then there was her mind—bruised by grief, fear, and the unbearable weight of dependence. The once vibrant girl who danced at weddings and laughed till her stomach hurt now flinched at her own reflection. She said she felt like "half a person."

Our work began not with the legs, but with the heart. I told her we wouldn't talk about walking—not yet. We would talk about freedom. Dignity. Choice.

We started with seated core engagement—activating her transverse abdominis and spinal stabilizers to improve trunk control. She learned to find her center of gravity and balance without leaning heavily to one side. Even the smallest muscle activation brought surprise to her face. "I can feel that," she whispered once, wide-eyed.

We progressed to upper limb strengthening—using resistance bands for scapular control, triceps, and shoulder muscles essential for independent transfers and wheelchair propulsion. Each repetition was framed not as an exercise but as a step toward reclaiming independence. The first time she managed to push herself up from the chair without help, her eyes shone. "I didn't think I could ever do that," she said.

One of the hardest parts was facing public spaces. She shared how she avoided going out because people either stared too much or didn't look at all. I encouraged her to start small—brief visits to familiar places. We worked on wheelchair maneuvering: improving her pushing technique, turning on different surfaces, and managing ramps—all evidence-based interventions for community reintegration in incomplete spinal cord injury.

Mat-based exercises focused on pelvic stability and gluteal activation to assist with balance and transfers. We introduced sit-to-supine and supine-to-sit transitions, both critical for floor recovery techniques.

We also incorporated supported standing using a standing frame and parallel bars—an essential strategy for maintaining bone density, cardiovascular health, and psychological well-being. Jessica expressed fear at first, but gradually began to tolerate upright posture for longer durations.

Breathing mechanics were not ignored. We taught diaphragmatic breathing to improve trunk stability and reduce spasticity, which is supported in neurorehabilitation research. Additionally, her spasticity was managed through gentle prolonged stretching, proper wheelchair seating adjustments, and muscle relaxation techniques.

Her mental well-being was a constant thread in our sessions. We framed setbacks as opportunities for adaptation rather than defeat. I also connected her to an online peer support group, which is recommended in SCI rehabilitation guidelines for social reintegration.

Her parents joined occasional sessions where we openly discussed the need for balancing care with independence. We worked on caregiver training for safe transfers and positioning—practical aspects that reduced their anxiety while empowering Jessica.

Months passed. Jessica returned one day wearing a bright maroon kurta, her hair styled, a quiet determination in her eyes. "I went to my cousin's wedding," she shared. "I wore heels just for the look." She laughed, tapping her wheelchair. "I sat the whole time, but I still wore them."

Her words carried quiet power: "I sat, but I still wore them."

Her progress wasn't about a miracle cure. It was about reclaiming identity, mobility, and self-worth—one adaptive technique, one conversation, one milestone at a time.

In our final session, she said softly: "I thought my life ended the day I lost my legs. But maybe... maybe I just started living differently."

The Curve

Healing isn't always about standing tall. Sometimes it's about finding new ways to move, new ways to belong, and most of all—new ways to see yourself. A life redefined is still a life worth living, no matter how the world chooses to see you.

TWENTY FIVE

THE ANXIOUS ENTREPRENEUR

Riya Mehta came to The Flexion like many I've met—on the surface, successful, sharp, and endlessly driven. But beneath that polished exterior, she was unraveling. The neck pain, the tight shoulders, the constant upper back tension—those were the symptoms. The real story was her anxiety. Her body wasn't just tired; it was bracing.

"I can't seem to switch off," she admitted during our first session. "Even when I'm resting, I'm not really resting. I'm always... wired."

I could see it in the way she sat—shoulders tense, breath shallow, eyes darting. Her mind never stopped, and neither did her body's stress response.

We began gently. Micro-movements. Guided breath resets. Postural awareness. It wasn't about big changes—it was about inviting her nervous system to feel safe enough to let go.

At first, the stillness was uncomfortable. She confessed once, "I'm so used to chasing the next thing, I don't know how to just... be."

But slowly, as her sessions unfolded, she softened. Her posture shifted. Her breath deepened. She began to smile more, to move with less bracing, to live without the constant hum of tension.

The Outcome

Riya's physical pain eased, but more importantly, she discovered how to pause without guilt. How to breathe without rushing. How to move not from fear, but from trust.

The Curve

Sometimes the hardest thing isn't moving forward—it's learning to stand still. Riya reminded me that healing isn't just for the body—it's for the mind that never stops running.

A Gentle Pause

We all carry silent stories about what our bodies can—or cannot—do.

What is one belief, one fear, that you've been holding onto about your strength, your movement, or your recovery?

What might it feel like to loosen that grip—just a little—and let something new unfold?

TWENTY SIX

THE GRANDMA WHO DIDN'T NEED PERMISSION TO MOVE

Mrs. Laxmi Rao arrived at The Flexion with the kind of energy that filled the room before she even sat down. At 74, she carried herself with unapologetic independence, the kind you earn through years of raising families, running homes, and never once waiting for someone to tell you what you could or couldn't do.

"I hurt my back," she said, waving her hand like it was an afterthought. "Lifting water. Don't tell me to rest, Doctor—I have things to do."

I smiled because I've met her type before: strong-willed, sharp-tongued, and utterly determined not to be slowed down by something as ordinary as pain.

We started gently. Functional movement. Breath-led mobility. Posture work designed not to limit her but to keep her doing what she loved safely. It wasn't about telling her to stop—it was about teaching her how to move better.

At first, she grumbled. "You physios take all the fun out of life," she joked. But session by session, she softened—not just physically, but in spirit. Her body learned to move without strain, and she began to trust it again.

One day, she brought me laddus. "Not sugar-free," she grinned. "But pain-free."

The Outcome

Mrs. Rao didn't give up her independence—she reclaimed it fully, armed with new knowledge and renewed confidence.

The Curve

Some people teach you as much as you help them. Mrs. Rao reminded me that strength isn't about never stumbling—it's about never surrendering your joy, your purpose, or your freedom to pain.

TWENTY SEVEN

THE GRIEVING WIDOW

Latha's world ended quietly one Sunday morning. A phone call. A collapsed husband. A life, forever altered.

After the funeral, the house emptied, but her grief stayed. She stopped stepping outside, stopped calling friends, stopped moving except when absolutely necessary. Her body grew heavy—not just with sorrow, but with stillness. Days turned into weeks. Weeks into months. And with them came a deep, relentless back pain that seemed as immovable as her sadness.

Her family doctor said, "You need to move." But Latha couldn't find the will. It was a neighbor—kind but persistent—who finally convinced her to try physiotherapy.

And that's how she met me.

Latha arrived at The Flexion slouched, her expression guarded, her eyes clouded by the kind of tiredness that sleep can't fix.

"I'm not here to push you," I told her gently. "But I can help you find your feet again—if you'll let me."

She offered a half-smile. "I don't think my body remembers how."

I nodded. "Then let's help it remember."

Her recovery didn't begin on a mat. It began with conversation. With witnessing her grief, not dismissing it. With teaching her that her pain wasn't just emotional—it was physical too. Muscles weaken. Joints stiffen. Breath shortens. The body, like the heart, can lock itself down after trauma.

We started small. Incredibly small. Just changing positions every hour. Standing by the window. Seated mobility. Bedside pelvic tilts. Calf pumps. Every gentle movement was framed not as "exercise" but as permission to live again.

I'd remind her:

"Imagine you're watering your plants again."

"Let's get you ready for those temple steps you loved."

Sometimes she laughed. Sometimes she cried. But she moved.The Outcome

Weeks passed. The pain didn't vanish, but it softened. Latha began to sit longer. Stand longer. Walk short distances without dread. One day, she surprised herself by walking to her local temple unaided. She told me, with quiet pride:

"It felt like reclaiming something I thought I'd lost."

Her family noticed too. She started wearing her sarees again. She baked her husband's favorite rava cake for the first time since he passed.

The Curve

Latha's recovery wasn't about chasing perfection. It wasn't about "getting over" her loss. It was about choosing life, movement, and moments—even when her heart was still healing.

Because sometimes, healing isn't loud. It's the quiet decision to stand up. To step outside. To let the body remember—and in doing so, let the heart follow.

TWENTY EIGHT

THE POST-SURGICAL DISAPPOINTMENT

Verma sat across from me with the look I've come to recognize—tired, frustrated, and quietly defeated. He was 47, nearly a year post-lumbar spine surgery, and yet the pain that was supposed to disappear hadn't.

"I did everything they told me," he said, his voice flat. "Bed rest, physio, back to work. But this nagging ache... some days, it's worse than before."

What weighed on him wasn't just the discomfort—it was the confusion. The feeling of being let down. The growing fear that maybe this was it: the new normal.

I listened. Carefully.

Surgery had addressed the disc, yes. But pain? Pain is more complex than scans. Sometimes the nervous system stays stuck, the body overprotects, and even after the structure is 'fixed,' the brain doesn't feel safe.

We shifted the focus from 'fixing' to 'retraining.'

We began gently. Breathwork. Mobility. Building awareness of movement patterns that had long been guarded. I reminded him: surgery didn't fail him—it just wasn't the full story.At first, Verma moved cautiously, afraid to bend, to trust his own body. But step by step, session by session, that fear softened.

By week four, he was walking without hesitation.

By week six, he was playing cricket with his son.

By week eight, he stopped talking about his back and started living again.

One day, he arrived with tea for both of us. He grinned. "I don't think about it all the time anymore."

I smiled. "That's the milestone I was waiting for."

The Outcome

Verma learned that healing isn't just about structural change—it's about movement, trust, and reclaiming life beyond fear.

The Curve

Some recoveries aren't about erasing pain entirely. They're about loosening its grip—until it fades quietly into the background, where it belongs.

TWENTY NINE

THE FLORIST WHO
STOOD AGAIN

Ramalakshmi was forty-eight, known in her small village of Kothapet for her radiant garlands and gentle smile. Nestled between lush green fields and bordered by a lazy river, Kothapet was the kind of place where time seemed to pause—where life revolved around the rhythm of the seasons, the village temple, and the simple joys of community.

For over twenty years, Ramalakshmi had run a modest flower stall just outside the gates of the ancient Vishnu temple at the heart of Kothapet. Her hands were deft, weaving jasmine, roses, and marigolds into fragrant offerings that devotees believed carried their prayers to the heavens. Her life was simple, sacred, and rooted in tradition. But when she came to The Flexion, she carried something far heavier than flower baskets.

She could barely walk without pain.

The problem had crept up slowly. First, an ache in the lower back after standing for long hours during festival seasons. Then a sharp, burning discomfort deep in the pelvis that radiates to her thighs. She had dismissed it as "overwork" or "age catching up," comforted by neighborhood remedies—herbal balms, temple blessings, and the occasional painkiller. But the pain grew bolder, forcing her to abandon the temple stall she so dearly loved.

When she spoke in our first session, her voice trembled: "Doctor garu, I don't want to stop my work. The temple, the flowers... it is my life."

Her clinical assessment pointed to Sacroiliac Joint Dysfunction—a condition often missed, misdiagnosed as lumbar disc pain or sciatica. Her SI joint was hypermobile, with muscle imbalances and poor pelvic stability compounding the issue. There were no alarming red flags, but the physical discomfort had been worsened by months of movement avoidance and deep-seated fear.

I could see how much her identity was intertwined with her work. It wasn't just about flowers—it was about faith, community, and being useful. Her eyes filled with tears when she described missing Ugadi and Vaikuntha Ekadashi—seasons when her garlands adorned hundreds of homes and deities.

We began, as always, with breath. Diaphragmatic breathing to reduce her nervous system's hypersensitivity, to calm the protective guarding around her pelvis. I reassured her: "We are not here to push through pain. We are here to rebuild trust—with your body, with movement, with life itself."

We started with non-weight-bearing exercises: gentle pelvic tilts in supine, glute activation without lumbar stress, and knee fall-outs to wake up deep stabilizers. I explained the concept of "form closure" and "force closure"—how ligaments and muscles together stabilize the SI joint.

She was cautious at first. Every time she felt the familiar twinge, her breath would catch. But with slow progressions—side-lying clamshells, resistance band glute bridges, and eventually standing pelvic control drills—she began to notice the difference. Less sharpness. More confidence.

Her cultural beliefs were deeply ingrained, and we wove them into her recovery. She timed her home exercises with the soft morning Suprabhatam chants from the temple. She counted her breath using her prayer beads. Healing, I reminded her, is not separate from life—it is part of it.

As her stability improved, we addressed her standing tolerance. We introduced step-ups, single-leg balance work, and gradual return to walking longer distances. She practiced gentle hip hinge patterns so she could bend to pick up flower baskets without fear of "damage." She learned the art of pacing—breaking her flower work into manageable time blocks.

One afternoon, she arrived beaming. "I made garlands for the Vishnu temple's Friday puja," she said, her voice full of life. "Not many, but I stood. I didn't feel scared."

Her smile told the story her words couldn't. The SI joint pain that had once defined her was no longer the center of her life. She had found herself again—not by returning to the exact past, but by embracing a future where movement and meaning coexisted.

In our final session, as she presented me with a small jasmine garland, she said softly: "I thought I was finished. But I remembered—the flower bloomed again, even after the storm."

The Curve

Sometimes healing is about more than fixing what hurts. It is about restoring the small rituals, the forgotten joys, the quiet dignity of standing tall in the life you love. And when that happens, pain becomes just one part of the story—not the whole of it.

THIRTY

THE CHIROPRACTIC DETOUR

Ravi was 52, a man who had spent years searching for an answer to his back pain. He'd seen it all—orthopedics, chiropractors, physiotherapists, each promising the elusive fix.

When he walked into The Flexion, he greeted me with a weary half-smile. "Let me guess, you're going to tell me to stretch and strengthen too?"

I smiled back. "Not until we understand the real story."

Ravi's back pain wasn't sudden. It had begun seven years earlier after a minor lifting injury. What started as a dull spasm became a cycle of stiffness, sharp episodes, and growing fear. He'd undergone every passive treatment imaginable: adjustments, stim, ultrasound, heat packs—each offering temporary relief but no lasting change.

The problem wasn't just his back—it was the belief that his back was fragile, permanently broken.

I listened. I asked him not just about the pain but about his thoughts around movement, fear, and trust.

"It feels like if I move wrong, something will snap," he confessed.

We started small: breathwork, gentle mobility, core reactivation. I explained how the body isn't made of glass—and how avoidance feeds pain.

Ravi was skeptical at first. Every flare-up rattled him. But he kept showing up.

By week four, he was walking longer. By week six, he was hiking with his family. By week eight, he stopped talking about his back and started talking about life.

One day, he arrived grinning. "I thought I needed someone to fix me. Turns out, I just needed someone to teach me how to move without fear."

The Outcome

Ravi didn't just recover—he reclaimed ownership of his body. The pain lessened. The confidence grew. And most importantly, the fear dissolved.

The Curve

Some recoveries aren't about magic hands or quick fixes. They're about slow, steady rewiring—of the body, of belief, of courage.

THIRTY ONE

THE SURVIVOR'S SECOND CHANCE

Desai was 55, and in many ways, already a survivor.

A year earlier, he had fought through colon cancer—surgery, chemotherapy, the works. The cancer was gone. The doctors declared him disease-free. But Desai? He didn't feel free.

"I thought I'd bounce back," he told me during his first visit. "But I feel like I've aged twenty years. My back hurts. My legs are weak. I can't even walk without stopping every few minutes."

He wasn't dealing with cancer anymore. He was dealing with the echoes it left behind.

Desai's scans were clear. His lab reports were normal. But his body had been through battle—and battles leave more than physical scars.

We started with breath. With simple movements. With the idea that progress wasn't about reclaiming who he was—it was about building who he could become.

The early sessions were humbling. Standing upright for ten minutes without fatigue became a milestone. Gentle spinal mobility, basic core engagement, slow but steady walking.

There were setbacks. Days when energy crashed. Moments when fear crept in—the haunting "what if it comes back?"

But Desai showed up. Again and again.

By week four, he walked to the corner store.

By week six, he returned to the family business.

By week eight, he was waking up not with dread, but with possibility.

One day, he shared quietly, "I used to wake up expecting pain. Now I wake up asking—what can I try today?"

The Outcome

Desai didn't just recover from cancer. He reclaimed his right to move, to live, to hope. His recovery wasn't about perfection. It was about presence.

The Curve

Some battles are fought on hospital beds. Others are fought quietly, every day, in the choice to move despite fear. Recovery isn't the absence of scars—it's the courage to build life beyond them.

Your Turn

Progress doesn't always look dramatic.

More often, it's quiet, subtle, and sometimes messy.

How can you begin to notice—and celebrate—the small, invisible victories along your own journey?

THIRTY TWO

THE MAN WHO LIFTED TOO MUCH

Prateek Kumar was thirty-six when his life changed in the blink of an eye. An avid fitness enthusiast and self-taught weightlifter, he was known in his social circle for his dedication to the gym. Every morning before sunrise, he could be found pushing his limits—deadlifts, squats, and power moves that he had learned from online videos and gym buddies.

But one morning, mid-rep during his usual deadlift session, he felt something he had never felt before: a sharp jolt of pain in his lower back that stopped him cold. It wasn't the usual post-workout soreness. It was something deeper. Sharper. A line had been crossed.

Within hours, the pain intensified. By evening, Prateek could barely stand upright. He felt shooting pain radiating down his left leg—a textbook radiculopathy, the kind that makes you wince with even the slightest movement. The next morning, he noticed tingling and weakness in his foot. That's when fear set in.

When he arrived at The Flexion, he was visibly distressed. "I don't understand," he said. "I've been working out for years. I thought I was strong."

His MRI confirmed the diagnosis: Acute lumbar disc prolapse at L4-L5 with nerve root compression. The disc had herniated laterally, pressing on the nerve roots that supply the lower limb. There were no prior warning signs—no history of minor backaches, no gradual stiffness. The injury had struck suddenly but decisively.

I explained the mechanism gently: repeated heavy lifting without proper core bracing or spinal alignment creates excessive intradiscal pressure. Without appropriate load management, muscular control, or protective technique, the spine's weakest link—the intervertebral disc—can fail catastrophically.

Prateek had never used a lifting belt. He had rarely scaled his weights down. "No pain, no gain," he admitted, half-smiling. "I thought that's how it works."

We began conservatively. His first priority was pain management and neural protection. He was advised to avoid any spinal loading. We focused on neural mobility (nerve gliding), gentle pelvic tilts, and diaphragmatic breathing to calm his overactive nervous system.

He struggled mentally. "I feel useless," he confessed during one session. "I can't sit, can't drive, can't even pick up my daughter."

We addressed not just his physical pain, but his identity crisis. The man who had defined himself through strength now faced helplessness. I reassured him: "Recovery isn't about who you were before. It's about who you're becoming now."

Gradually, as his radicular pain eased, we introduced McKenzie extension protocols—a well-researched method for lumbar discogenic pain. He practiced prone lying, then prone on elbows, progressing to press-ups as tolerated.

His mobility improved. We layered in core stability—not heavy lifts, but slow, controlled activation of the transverse abdominis, multifidus, and gluteal muscles. Bridges, bird-dogs, dead bugs—movements that seemed simple but demanded precision.

By the third month, we introduced isometric holds, bodyweight squats, and hip-hinge retraining. He learned for the first time that lifting wasn't just about muscles—it was about form, breath, timing, and awareness. He used a mirror to correct his posture, incorporated mobility drills for his hips and thoracic spine, and, most importantly, respected his body's new boundaries.

One day, after successfully completing a set of hip hinges without pain, he smiled and said: "I used to think strength was in how much I could lift. Now I know—it's in how much I can move well."

In our final phase, we reintroduced light deadlifts with strict form, reduced load, and a proper lifting belt. He practiced neutral spine positioning, breath control, and bracing techniques that protected his lumbar discs. He was cautious, but no longer fearful.

The Curve

Pain is sometimes the body's way of calling us back to wisdom. Strength without control is fragile. Recovery is not about chasing the past—it's about rebuilding on a foundation of respect, knowledge, and the quiet confidence that comes from moving well, not just lifting heavy.

THIRTY THREE

THE CODER WHO DEBUGGED HIS SPINE

Karthik was 32, fluent in four programming languages but clueless about one thing: his own body.

He came to The Flexion looking defeated, clutching an MRI report like it was a resignation letter. "L5-S1 disc bulge," he muttered. "Doctor says if this doesn't improve, I'll need surgery."

His eyes were tired—panic just beneath the surface. He wasn't just worried about his back. He was terrified of losing everything his career represented: identity, stability, pride.

We sat down and started where I always start: the story.

"I spend 10–12 hours a day coding," he explained. "I sit, I stress, I barely move."

I nodded. "Your body isn't broken, Karthik. It's just stuck. Let's teach it to move again."

His assessment revealed the usual culprits: tight hips, sleepy glutes, a core that hadn't seen action since his college cricket days. But more than that, I saw fear—every movement laced with the question: Will this hurt me more?We began slowly: breathwork to calm his system, gentle nerve glides, foundational strength.

Week one was rough. So was week two. He confessed he almost gave up.

But then... something shifted. He began to trust. To notice the tiny wins.

By week four, he was sitting longer without pain. By week six, he walked three kilometers. By week eight, he cancelled the surgical consultation.

One day, he showed me his phone wallpaper: a cartoon of a spine with a cape. He smiled. "My new superhero."

I laughed. "Looks like you debugged more than just code."

The Outcome

Karthik didn't just dodge surgery. He rebuilt trust—in his body, in movement, in the idea that healing isn't just possible—it's personal.

The Curve

Sometimes the solution isn't to overhaul everything. It's to find the faulty line, breathe, and rewrite the pattern—slowly, kindly, one step at a time.

Carrying On While Caring

Anita was 45, a full-time caregiver to her mother, who had been paralyzed after a stroke two years earlier.

Her days were built around lifting, shifting, feeding, bathing—tasks that left no room for rest. There were no weekends off. No sick days. No space to say, "I need help."

Her back pain wasn't sudden. It crept in—the dull ache after long days, the sharp jabs after awkward lifts, the exhaustion that settled deep into her bones. But every morning, she rose and carried on. Because she had to.

When Anita came to me, she wasn't looking for miracles.

"I don't need to be perfect, Doctor," she said quietly. "I just need to not break down."

We started gently. Breathwork. Awareness. Small movements designed to ease the burden she bore—not just physically, but mentally. We worked on how to lift her mother safely, how to pause without guilt, how to rebuild strength that had long been running on empty.

Her pain reduced. Not entirely. But enough to breathe again.

Some days still hurt. Some days were better. But Anita had learned something powerful: asking for help isn't weakness. Micro-breaks matter. She deserved care too.

She still carries her mother. But she also carries herself—differently, gently, with more kindness.

Her recovery isn't finished. But her resilience? It shines.

THIRTY FOUR

THE DESK SLAVE WHO ESCAPED THE DIGITAL PRISON

Kunal was twenty-seven and living what most people his age would call "the dream."

A rising star at one of Hyderabad's top tech firms, he coded for hours, led international projects, and squeezed in late-night gaming marathons. His life revolved around screens: laptops, monitors, phones, tablets—sometimes all at once.

Until one morning, his back gave out.

The pain had started subtly: a mild ache after long hours of sitting, stiffness when standing. But that day, as he bent to pick up his charger, a sharp jolt dropped him to his knees. Panic took hold.

An MRI showed a disc bulge. The advice was predictable: rest, painkillers, and if things worsened—surgery.

That word—surgery—sent him spiraling.

He tried everything: lumbar belts, YouTube stretches, standing desks, online consultations. But the pain persisted. Worse still, it began to chip away at his mind. He felt anxious, irritable, disconnected. His world—once limitless within screens—felt like it was closing in.

A friend finally nudged him toward The Flexion.

When I met Kunal, he looked exhausted—physically and emotionally.

I smiled gently. "How long have you been trapped in this digital prison?"

He blinked. "Feels like forever."

We began not with fear but with understanding. His scans weren't the problem—his patterns were. Hours of sitting, shallow breathing, deactivated core, immobile hips. His body wasn't broken. It was simply stuck.

We started with breathwork. Short mobility drills. Gentle core engagement. I asked him to take micro-breaks—not just for his spine, but for his mind.

He groaned at first. "I live on screens," he protested.

I smiled. "Then let's teach your body to live too."

Progress came in layers. By week three, he felt steadier. By week six, he was coding without pain.

By week eight, he went for his first screen-free walk in months.

In his final session, he said quietly, "I thought my mind was my greatest asset. But I forgot it needs a body to carry it."

I nodded. "Brains need movement too."

The Outcome

Kunal didn't just recover from back pain. He rewrote the story of how he lived—learning that true productivity begins with presence, not pressure.

The Curve

Sometimes the biggest escape isn't from an office or a device—it's from the habits that quietly trap us. Movement isn't optional. It's how we come back to life.

THIRTY FIVE

THE RUNNER WHO COULDN'T STOP

Chandrakant was twenty-nine when his body forced him to a halt he never saw coming. A software engineer by profession and a runner by passion, he had built his identity around movement. Early morning jogs, weekend marathons, charity runs—running was not just exercise, it was who he was.

So when pain crept into his left buttock and down the back of his thigh, he brushed it off as overuse. "Just tightness," he told himself. He stretched, foam-rolled, pushed through. But the discomfort escalated—turning into sharp, burning pain that worsened with every run, every hill, every attempt to do the thing he loved most.

When he came to The Flexion, he hadn't run in over three months. "I feel like I've lost myself," he said quietly. "The races, the running groups, even my mornings—it's all gone."

His scans were clean. No lumbar disc prolapse. No nerve compression. No SI joint dysfunction. Yet the pain persisted stubbornly, localized around the gluteal region and occasionally radiating along the posterior thigh—classic signs of gluteal tendinopathy with piriformis involvement, commonly mistaken for sciatica.

I explained the mechanism: chronic overload, poor lateral hip control, and muscle imbalances from excessive mileage without cross-training. His gluteus medius and deep rotators were fatigued beyond their capacity. The pain wasn't "all in his head"—it was his body's signal that something had to change.

We began by pulling him out of the pain cycle. Step one: complete rest from running, but not from movement. We initiated isometric gluteal loading—bridges held for time, side-lying hip abductions, gentle nerve mobility without provoking symptoms.

"But if I don't run, who am I?" he asked once, blinking back frustration. This wasn't just physical. Like many athletes, his self-worth was deeply intertwined with his sport. Losing running felt like losing his place in the world.

I reassured him: "You're not just the miles you log. Healing doesn't mean giving up—it means recalibrating."

As his pain reduced, we introduced eccentric glute strengthening, step-down drills, and single-leg stability work. He learned that rehab wasn't about passivity—it was active, deliberate, and, in many ways, more demanding than his previous training.

We also corrected his biomechanics: tight hip flexors, poor thoracic mobility, and weak lateral core muscles that fed into faulty running mechanics. He learned dynamic stretches, running-specific strength, and pacing—tools he had never valued before.

By the sixth week, his confidence returned. Short walks became slow jogs. Slow jogs became interval sessions. I emphasized load management: not chasing distance or speed, but building resilience gradually.

One morning, after completing his first pain-free 5K in nearly six months, he came to the clinic grinning. "I thought I had to run to prove something," he said. "Now I just run because I can."

The Curve

Sometimes the hardest lesson for those who love movement is learning to pause. Pain is not failure—it's feedback. And recovery is not the end of a journey, but the beginning of a wiser one. When we learn to move not to escape, but to reconnect, we find freedom that lasts.

THIRTY SIX

THE TEEN WHO LEARNED TO STAND FOR HIMSELF

Rishi was just sixteen, but the way he moved made him look older—shoulders slouched, head forward, spine weighed down by something more than books.

He came to The Flexion with his mother, both of them unsure of what to expect. "It's probably bad posture," she said apologetically. "He's always on his phone or laptop."

But when I sat with Rishi, I noticed something else—the silence, the hesitation, the way his eyes avoided mine when I asked, "When did the pain start?"

"It's been months," he mumbled. "Some days it's okay. Some days it just... hurts everywhere."

His scans were clear. His body, however, was telling a different story: tight chest, weak core, locked upper back. But deeper still was something I see far too often in teens—pressure. Expectations. The quiet weight of never feeling enough.

"You're not just carrying a backpack," I told him gently. "You're carrying everything you don't say out loud."

He looked up, startled, then softened.

We started small: breathwork, gentle thoracic mobility, hip activation. Nothing fancy. Just reminders to his body—and his mind—that it was safe to move.

Week by week, he grew steadier. His breath deepened. His posture lifted. I watched his eyes change first—less guarded, more present.

One morning, he arrived early, unprompted, and helped me set up mats. That's when I knew something had shifted.

At the end of his final session, he handed me his old backpack. Inside was a note: "I've learned to carry myself differently now. Thank you for helping me find that."

I kept that backpack. It reminds me that sometimes the heaviest loads aren't physical.

The Outcome

Rishi didn't just find relief from his back pain— he found confidence. He learned that standing tall isn't just about the spine—it's about how you carry yourself through life.

The Curve

Some of the most powerful recoveries happen quietly. One breath, one movement, one decision to rise—not just physically, but fully.

THIRTY SEVEN

THE GIRL WHO REFUSED THE SURGERY

Ananya was twenty-three. Young, radiant, and alive in movement. Dance wasn't just something she loved—it was who she was. Bharatanatyam, contemporary, freestyle—her body told stories her words never could.

Until one day, her back said no.

There was no dramatic fall. No heroic injury. Just a slow, creeping pain that began in her lower back and spread down her leg, until even the act of standing felt fragile.

The MRI brought the verdict: L4-L5 disc bulge with nerve compression.

The first orthopedic appointment was brief. Clinical. "You'll need surgery," the doctor announced, without looking up. "Sooner rather than later."

Ananya's world collapsed. "I'm only twenty-three," she whispered to me when we first met. "Dance is... everything."

Her voice was soft, but her eyes screamed fear.

I nodded gently. "Then let's start by changing the story your body believes."We began slowly—deliberately. Breathwork. Pelvic control. Gentle mobility. No grand leaps. Just small, steady movements designed to calm the nervous system and rebuild trust.

Some days she doubted. Some days she cried. But she kept showing up.

By week four, her limp was gone.

By week six, she danced—just for five minutes, but she moved.

By week eight, she danced without fear.

The Outcome

Ananya didn't just avoid surgery—she reclaimed her movement, her confidence, and her identity. She learned that healing wasn't about perfection. It was about possibility.

The Curve

Some recoveries aren't about erasing every trace of pain. They're about returning to the things we love—one breath, one step, one gentle motion at a time.

Ananya's curve didn't just change. It let her dance again.

THIRTY EIGHT

THE BOY WHO CARRIED HIS HOMETOWN ON HIS BACK

Chakravarthy was nineteen, and in the eyes of his small village near Warangal, he was already a champion. A national-level weightlifter with dreams stitched tightly to every muscle and bone in his body, he carried more than just iron bars—he carried the hopes of his family, his town, and the countless eyes that saw in him a ticket to pride and recognition.

When he came to The Flexion, though, he was broken—not by injury alone, but by fear.

It started without warning. A sharp, searing pain in his mid-back during a routine clean-and-jerk session. He had lifted heavier before. He had trained harder before. But this time, something was different. The pain didn't fade. It worsened, creeping into his sleep, making every breath, every twist, a grimace of discomfort.

His local coach told him it was just muscle strain. He tried rest, liniments, massages. But the pain persisted. When he finally arrived in my clinic, he could barely manage a full breath without flinching.

We began with a thorough examination. There was tenderness along his thoracic spine, limited extension, but no red-flag neurological deficits. Still, something felt off—an intuition honed by years of seeing what others miss. I suggested imaging.

The MRI revealed the truth: a Butterfly Vertebra at T8—a rare congenital anomaly where the vertebral body is split, leaving a wedge-like gap. For years it had gone unnoticed, his body compensating until the demands of elite-level lifting pushed it beyond its limits. There was no fracture, no disc herniation—but the anomaly explained his instability, his pain, and his sudden breakdown.

When we shared the news, Chakravarthy's face crumbled. "Does this mean I can't lift anymore?" he whispered. His eyes searched mine, desperate.

I knew this was more than a medical discussion—it was the potential death of a dream. In small towns like his, sport isn't just a pastime. It's a way out. A source of dignity. An identity.

I explained everything gently. The anomaly was real, but it wasn't a sentence to immobility. With careful load management, biomechanical retraining, and dedicated physiotherapy, he could return—not recklessly, but wisely. The risk could be managed. His body could be fortified.

We started with thoracic mobility, scapular control, and core endurance training. Gone were the days of lifting heavy without preparation. He learned diaphragmatic breathing, spinal control in all planes, and, most importantly, the art of respecting his own limits.

Emotionally, it was a battle. He struggled with guilt—feeling he had let down not just himself but his village. The boy who once moved like lightning on the platform now moved with hesitation.

Week by week, though, something shifted. His strength returned—but so did his wisdom. He learned to listen to his body. He became a student not just of sport, but of movement.

By the third month, we cautiously reintroduced light Olympic lifts with modified technique—shorter ranges, precise control, never chasing the old numbers. His pain faded. His confidence grew.

In his last session before returning home, he said something I'll never forget: "I used to think lifting was about how much weight you can carry. Now I know—it's about how much you can carry without losing yourself."

The Curve

Sometimes the heaviest burdens we carry are the expectations we place on ourselves. True strength is not the weight on the bar but the wisdom to know when to lift, when to pause, and how to rise again—not just as an athlete, but as a human being.

THIRTY NINE

THE BRUSH THAT FROZE

I first met Maya when she walked into The Flexion clutching her forearm, her fingers stiff, her posture guarded. She was 34—a painter whose hands had shaped color and canvas for years. But pain had slowly stolen her art.

"It started with a dull ache," she explained. "Then my back. My shoulder. Even holding the brush became impossible."

She smiled faintly as she spoke, but her eyes betrayed the fear. It wasn't just her body that hurt—it was the identity she felt slipping away.

I've seen it before: when the pain isn't just physical but tangled with the deepest parts of who we are.

We began where all recovery should begin: with reassurance. Her MRI wasn't a life sentence. Her nerves weren't broken. What her body needed was not avoidance, but safe movement and trust.

We didn't jump into aggressive exercises. We started small: gentle mobility, breathwork, core awareness. Movements that felt subtle, but for Maya, they were the first strokes of a new canvas.

Some days she wanted to give up. Some days the frustration of limitation overwhelmed her. But she kept showing up.

By week four, she painted for the first time without flinching.

By week six, she laughed while describing how she lost track of time in her studio again.

By week eight, her back no longer defined her day.

One afternoon, she looked at me with tears in her eyes and said, "I thought I'd lost her—the version of me who painted. But she's still here."

I nodded. "She was never gone. Just waiting for you to move differently."

The Outcome

Maya didn't just regain the use of her brush. She reclaimed her spirit. Her pain softened, her movements flowed, and her creativity returned—not by forcing her body, but by learning to trust it again.

The Curve

Some recoveries aren't loud. They happen quietly—in colors, in breath, in the simple joy of doing what we love. And sometimes the most important thing we regain isn't movement—it's ourselves.

FOURTY

THE MOUNTAIN TREKKER WHO REFUSED TO GIVE UP

For Meera, the mountains weren't just weekend getaways—they were home. At fifty-four, she had trekked nearly every peak in her state. From dense forests to wind-whipped cliffs, her heart belonged to the trails.

Her friends often joked that she wasn't aging—she was ascending.

Until the day her back said otherwise.

It started subtly: a dull ache in her lower spine during a casual hike. She brushed it off as one of those "old bones" moments. But the pain lingered. Steep ascents sent sharp jolts down her leg. Even descents felt unsteady. Soon, just lacing up her trekking boots triggered fear.

One afternoon, after cutting short a trail she could once conquer blindfolded, Meera sat on a rock and cried—not from physical pain, but from the creeping dread that her mountain days were over.

Her doctor's words made it worse: "Slipped disc. Nerve irritation. Better avoid strain. Time to slow down."

To Meera, that sounded like a life sentence.

A niece finally intervened. "You need someone who won't just tell you to stop living," she said, handing over a card for The Flexion.

The Journey Back

Meera didn't know what to expect on her first visit. Machines? Lectures? More warnings?

Instead, she found herself greeted by Dr. Yash, who asked her a question no one else had:

"What do the mountains mean to you?"

She blinked. "They make me feel... unafraid. Alive."

"Then let's help you get back there," he said simply.

The sessions didn't begin with heavy exercises. They began with listening. Breathwork. Gentle mobility. Small core activations. Each movement was framed not as "therapy" but as a return to trust—trust in her body, trust in herself.

Some days were tough. There were setbacks, frustration, even tears. But Meera kept showing up.

She began to notice how much tension she carried even when still. How shallow her breathing had become. How stiff and guarded her hips felt.

Session by session, she moved a little further. Walked a little taller. Believed a little more.

One day, she returned to her favorite trail—not for a summit, but for a simple walk. No fanfare. No pressure. Just the joy of movement. She wept, not from pain, but from the quiet freedom of it.

The Outcome

By week eight, Meera wasn't just moving without fear—she was living differently. She hadn't climbed her biggest mountain yet, but she knew she would. And for the first time in months, she felt unafraid.

The Curve

Sometimes the mountains we face aren't made of stone—they're made of fear, doubt, and stories that say we're too old, too fragile, too late.

But bodies, like mountains, are meant to be met—not conquered. When we stop fighting them and start listening, everything shifts.

Meera's story reminds us: the climb is still ours to make.

FORTY ONE

THE MAN WHO FOUND RELIEF WITHOUT ANSWERS

Basith was forty-one when he walked into The Flexion, carrying with him a thick folder of medical reports and a look of quiet defeat. The tests had all been done. MRI, CT scans, blood work, even nerve conduction studies. Every paper told him the same thing: "Nothing significant was found."

Yet his pain was very real.

For nearly a year, Basith had lived with unrelenting lower back pain. It had started subtly—an ache after long hours at his desk—but soon morphed into a constant discomfort that robbed him of sleep, drained his energy, and slowly eroded his confidence. He had consulted orthopaedic surgeons, neurologists, physiotherapists, and alternative medicine practitioners. Each one offered theories—muscle spasm, early degeneration, stress—but no clear diagnosis ever emerged.

"I sometimes feel like people think I'm imagining this," he admitted quietly in our first session. "I've done everything they asked. Scans show nothing. But the pain is always there."

His movement patterns were telling. He moved stiffly, guarding his lower back with every step, every transition from sitting to standing. Fear of movement—kinesiophobia—had crept in unnoticed. Like many patients with non-specific low back pain, Basith had become trapped in a cycle: pain led to fear, fear led to stiffness, stiffness fueled more pain.

I reassured him: "The absence of a clear diagnosis doesn't mean the pain isn't real. It just means that the problem isn't something structural we can see on a scan. But there is always something we can work on."

We began gently. The first goal wasn't to 'fix' anything—it was to move without fear. We started with diaphragmatic breathing, teaching him how to engage his core softly without over-bracing. Supine pelvic tilts became the first step in reminding his nervous system that movement could feel safe.

In the first two weeks, we kept everything simple: supported cat-camel movements, side-lying lumbar rotations, and walking short distances. Basith was skeptical. "How is this going to help if the pain is still there?" he asked during his third session.

I explained the science behind persistent pain—how sometimes the brain and nervous system stay on high alert long after the original issue has settled. I spoke to him about central sensitization, how fear and avoidance can amplify pain signals, and how graded exposure to movement helps retrain the system.

Basith listened carefully. It was the first time, he said, that someone had explained his situation without dismissing it as 'just stress' or 'nothing wrong.'

In the second month, we progressed. Basith began performing bridging exercises, resisted clamshells for glute activation, and standing mini squats. We used elastic bands to build gentle strength through his hips and core. His walking distance improved from 5 to 20 minutes without aggravating symptoms. He began to notice small but significant changes: better sleep, fewer sharp episodes, a gradual return of confidence.

I also addressed his sitting habits, introducing postural variability instead of rigid "perfect posture"—explaining that no single posture was harmful, but sustained positions without movement often were. This subtle shift in thinking helped him let go of the fear that every wrong move could cause damage.

In parallel, we incorporated basic mindfulness: simple body scanning techniques, breath awareness, and visual imagery during movements. Research supports the role of mindfulness in persistent pain, helping to lower threat perception and improve tolerance to activity.

By the third month, Basith was not only moving better—he was living better. He returned to his morning walks. He started attending social gatherings he had avoided. The pain was still present at times, but it no longer controlled his choices.

In one session, he shared: "I used to think I needed a diagnosis to heal. But maybe I just needed to stop waiting for an answer and start living again."

We introduced light resistance training in standing—banded rows, modified deadlifts, step-ups. Each exercise was scaled to his comfort, with the emphasis on form, breath, and progression. His gait became more fluid. His smile returned.

We never did find a clear diagnosis. And that was okay. Because not all healing requires an exact label. With time, patience, movement, and understanding, Basith's nervous system calmed. His muscles regained strength. His mind reclaimed hope.

In our final session, I asked him what had changed most. He thought for a moment, then said: "I stopped waiting for someone to fix me. I started trusting that I could help myself."

The Curve

Some recoveries don't come with clear answers. Sometimes the scans are clean, the blood tests normal, and still the pain persists. But movement, hope, and small daily victories can shift even the most stubborn pain. Because healing isn't always about finding the cause. Sometimes it's about finding the courage to move forward anyway.

FORTY TWO

THE WOMAN WHO CARRIED TRAUMA IN HER SPINE

For years, Pallavi believed she just had a "weak back."

She was 42, a successful HR manager, a mother of two, and the person everyone at home and work leaned on when life got messy. She was the fixer, the listener, the problem-solver.

And yet, she couldn't fix the one thing that affected her every single day: the constant, nagging ache in her lower back.

At first, it was manageable—occasional twinges after long hours at her desk or after a stressful family gathering. But gradually, the pain became her shadow. Mornings felt heavy. Bending over to tie her shoes triggered sharp discomfort. She began to withdraw—from social events, from evening walks, even from her children's playful demands.

Medical visits became routine. "Muscle strain," one doctor said. "Degenerative changes," said another. She was prescribed painkillers, told to rest, and warned to avoid lifting.

No one asked her about her life.

No one asked her about her story.

Until she came to The Flexion.

Pallavi smiled awkwardly during her first session. "Honestly, I'm not even sure why I'm here. I've tried everything."

I smiled gently. "Sometimes it's not about trying harder. It's about looking deeper."

We started not with machines or intense exercises—but with a conversation. How she stood. How she breathed. How she carried her stress.

And then came the question that changed everything:

"Has there been a time when your body felt unsafe?"

Her eyes widened. Memories surfaced—childhood struggles, years of caregiving for her unwell parents, a toxic relationship that had left scars deeper than skin. Things she had packed away long ago—except her body hadn't.

Her posture, her breath, her tension—they all held the story.

We moved gently. Breathing. Awareness. Subtle mobility drills that felt more like an invitation to safety than an exercise plan. Some sessions brought tears. Others brought laughter. But all brought something essential: presence.

One morning, weeks into her recovery, she caught herself humming while making tea—something she hadn't done in years. The pain hadn't vanished, but it no longer dictated her life.

She stood differently. Walked differently. And more importantly, she began living differently.

In her last session, Pallavi whispered, "I thought my back was weak. But I see now—I was just tired of carrying everything I never let go of."

I nodded. "When the body feels safe, it remembers how to heal."

The Outcome

Pallavi's back didn't just change because she moved differently. It changed because she lived differently. Her healing came not from fixing, but from softening—mentally, emotionally, physically.

The Curve

Some burdens don't show up on scans.

We carry old fears, hidden hurts, and silent stories not just in our minds but in our muscles, breath, and bones. Healing isn't always about doing more—it's about letting go.

When we feel safe in our own skin, we remember how to move, to breathe, and to trust again.

FORTY THREE

THE HOUSEWIFE WHO LIFTED HER LIFE WITH HER SPINE

Meena was 51, a quiet, soft-spoken woman whose life had always been about others. Cooking, cleaning, caring—her world revolved around her family, with barely a moment left for herself.

She came to The Flexion because of her back. But what she was really carrying wasn't just physical pain—it was the weight of years of silent service.

"It started with stiffness," she told me. "Then the pain. I thought it was just age. So I ignored it. But now... even simple things hurt. I can't kneel. I can't sweep. Even temple visits are difficult."

Her MRI showed mild degenerative changes, but her story showed something deeper: a life where her needs had always come last.

When I asked her when she last took time for herself, she laughed nervously. "I don't remember," she said. "There's always something to do."

We didn't start with complicated exercises. We started with breath. With gentle movement. With teaching her that her body wasn't broken—it was just asking for attention.

Session by session, Meena moved differently. Stood differently. Even spoke differently. The pain eased, not overnight, but gradually—as her body and her mind remembered what it felt like to belong to herself, too.

By week six, she smiled more. She moved without fear. She told me she'd begun taking short walks in the evenings—alone, by choice, for the first time in decades.

One day, she brought me a small box of sweets. "I lifted all the groceries myself this morning," she beamed. "And I'm not in pain."

We both laughed. It wasn't about groceries. It was about freedom.

The Outcome

Meena reclaimed not just her back, but her space in the world. Her movements grew steadier, her confidence brighter, and her life, just a little more hers again.

The Curve

Some recoveries are quiet revolutions. They happen not in grand leaps but in small acts—of movement, of self-care, of finally saying, "I matter too."

Meena's story reminded me: sometimes the weight we need to lift isn't outside us—it's the one we carry within.

FORTY FOUR

THE LIBRARIAN WHO FEARED TURNING PAGES

Lakshmi was sixty-two, a quiet woman who had spent nearly four decades in the service of books. She was the chief librarian of a small government library tucked into one of Hyderabad's older neighborhoods, a place where time moved slowly and the scent of old paper lingered in the air.

When she first came to The Flexion, she cradled her right arm gently, her neck stiff, her face carrying the weariness of someone who had grown used to discomfort. "It's the same pain every day," she said softly. "It starts from here..."—she touched her neck—"...and goes down to my hand. Even lifting books is difficult now."

She had seen two doctors. Both had offered painkillers. No scans were done. She had been told it was "age-related." So she adapted, as she always had: fewer books lifted, fewer shelves arranged, fewer walks to the temple. But the pain remained—

persistent, nagging, now accompanied by tingling in her fingers.

Her case was classic: a combination of cervical radiculopathy from mild spondylotic changes and thoracic outlet syndrome-like symptoms from years of forward head posture, shoulder rounding, and repetitive movements. Her scan, which I recommended gently, showed mild disc bulges at C5-C6, degenerative changes, and no red flags.

Lakshmi's pain wasn't just mechanical—it was emotional too. Her identity was tied to her role: the woman who kept the shelves neat, who guided children to books, who believed in the quiet power of knowledge. Losing the ability to turn pages without pain felt like losing herself.

We started gently. Her nervous system was sensitized, her posture protective. The first few sessions focused on cervical mobility within comfort, scapular retraction exercises, and diaphragmatic breathing to ease her habitual tension.

I taught her nerve gliding exercises for the brachial plexus—delicate, rhythmic movements to calm the irritated nerves without triggering symptoms. She practiced gentle chin tucks against the wall, and we worked on isometric neck holds to build confidence without strain.

Lakshmi was meticulous. Each session she noted down the exercises carefully, just as she once catalogued books. She asked questions about science—curious in the quiet, thoughtful way that suited her. "Is it really okay to move?" she asked once, visibly anxious.

I explained that movement was not the enemy. Inactivity, fear, and long-held tension were more harmful. I showed her research on graded exposure, on how tissue healing and nervous system recalibration take time, not avoidance.

As her mobility improved, we added resistance band rows, wall angels, and light overhead reaches. Her grip strength, once weakened by nerve irritation, began to return. We also addressed her workspace: adjusted the desk height at the library, taught her to alternate tasks, and emphasized micro-breaks.

The real change, however, wasn't just in her neck or shoulder—it was in her voice. In one session, she smiled and said, "I arranged the children's section yesterday. The books were heavy, but I managed. And I wasn't afraid."

We gradually progressed to thoracic mobility drills, simple functional lifts, and longer walking sessions. She regained the freedom to move her head, lift without flinching, and even resumed light gardening at home—something she had abandoned years earlier.

In our final session, Lakshmi sat upright, her shoulders relaxed, her eyes brighter. "The books are still there," she said, laughing softly. "And I can turn the pages again."

The Curve

Healing isn't always about grand gestures. Sometimes it's about the quiet return of simple freedoms: turning a page, lifting a book, walking without fear. And in those small victories, life reclaims its color—one careful movement at a time.

FORTY FIVE

THE CEO WHO LEARNED THAT HUSTLE NEEDS A CORE

Aarav had built three apps, raised two rounds of funding, and slept less than four hours a night—all before he turned 30. His life revolved around caffeine, calendar blocks, and chaos. His motto? "Sleep is for after the IPO."

His laptop was his best friend. His chair? An afterthought. Movement? A luxury.

So when he first felt a sharp sting in his lower back after a pitch meeting, he brushed it off. "Just a tweak. I'll stretch later."

He didn't.

The pain became a guest who overstayed— showing up during flights, while driving, even mid-presentation. He started using a lumbar pillow. Then a belt. Then painkillers. But one morning, as he leaned forward to tie his shoes, his back locked.

He couldn't stand back up. His back had filed a formal protest.

That's when a concerned friend nudged him toward The Flexion.

"I don't have time for long treatments," Aarav told me in our first meeting.

I smiled. "Then let's stop wasting time with shortcuts."

The assessment felt like a board meeting—but for his body. Every weak link was exposed: tight hip flexors, inhibited glutes, poor thoracic mobility, a core that had been outsourced to caffeine and denial.

"You've optimized your company," I told him. "Now let's optimize the one machine you can't replace."

He chuckled—carefully.

Our sessions became his refuge. One hour where breath mattered more than backlogs. Where posture mattered more than profits.

Aarav learned to brace before lifting—not just weights, but even thoughts. He practiced alignment, mobility, and breathing—not to impress anyone, but to reclaim himself.

By week three, he was sleeping better.

By week five, his pain had reduced by 80%.

By week seven, he canceled the spine surgery consultation.

He even started encouraging his team to take walking meetings.

In his final session, Aarav gifted us a smart clock that reminded people to move. Attached to it was a small note:

"Thanks for debugging my back before I crashed entirely."

I smiled.

Another high-performer had finally learned that hustle means nothing if your spine quits early.

What Aarav rebuilt wasn't just his back—it was his belief that life could still be climbed, slowly, steadily, his way.

The Outcome

Aarav didn't just dodge surgery—he redefined success. He discovered that ambition without alignment is a recipe for burnout, and that progress doesn't always mean pushing harder.

The Curve

Sometimes the breakthrough isn't in the boardroom or the balance sheet—it's in the quiet decision to move differently, to value the body as much as the mind, and to step back just enough to keep stepping forward.

A Moment of Realization:

Physiotherapy didn't just ease their pain.

It gave them back something far more powerful—their voice.

The freedom to choose movement over fear.

The confidence to rewrite stories that once felt written in stone.

Tilling Through Pain

Mahesh was 49—a farmer, a father, and the kind of man whose hands told stories of years spent tilling the land. He arrived at The Flexion with quiet eyes, his movements stiff, his voice low.

"I've always had back pain," he said, almost casually, as if it was just another season of life he had learned to live with.

His work didn't stop because of discomfort. The fields demanded him, rain or shine, with or without pain. But over time, what began as mild stiffness had grown into sharp twinges with every bend, every lift, every harvest.

He didn't come to me asking for miracles. He came because he was tired of bracing for pain at every sunrise.

We started with gentle mobility—small drills that seemed almost too simple for someone who worked the earth daily. We focused on breath, on core stability, on releasing the tightness that years of labor had layered into his spine.

Progress came slowly. Some days, he moved with ease. Other days, the pain crept back, stubborn as old soil. But Mahesh kept showing up, his dedication unshaken.

He learned how to lift differently. How to move with more awareness. How to breathe through the strain instead of bracing against it.

The pain didn't vanish. But Mahesh's fear of it—his helplessness in the face of it—did.

One afternoon, after weeks of steady work, he smiled faintly and said, "I still hurt sometimes. But I don't feel broken anymore."

He returned to his fields. To his life. To the rhythm of the land. Not fully pain-free. But no longer trapped by it.

His recovery is still unfolding. His story is still being written.

FORTY SIX

THE MOTHER WHO REBUILT HERSELF BEFORE HER CHILD NOTICED

Sneha came to me eight months after giving birth, carrying not just her baby but the invisible weight of exhaustion, discomfort, and self-doubt.

Her baby had begun sleeping through the night, but she hadn't. Her back ached. Her shoulders burned. Her neck protested every time she fed or lifted her child. Yet she told herself it was "normal." Everyone around her said the same.

"It'll get better," they assured her.

But it wasn't.

Sneha had tried everything: YouTube yoga, postpartum core challenges, turmeric milk. Some things helped briefly, others made her feel worse. Her smile was polite, but her eyes told me what her words didn't: she was tired—tired of hurting, tired of feeling trapped in a body she no longer recognized.

I didn't rush. I listened.

I asked about her delivery. Her feeding positions. Her daily routines. Her sleep—or the lack of it. I asked not just about her body but about her life.

Her physical assessment revealed what many new mothers face but rarely voice: weakened deep core, stressed shoulders, neglected glutes, and a nervous system running on overdrive.

"You've been lifting your baby with love," I told her gently, "but without the right muscle support."

Her eyes welled up.

We began quietly—simple breathwork, deep core reactivation, gentle thoracic mobility. Each movement wasn't just physical; it was an invitation for Sneha to return to her own body with kindness.

She learned that postpartum isn't a phase. It's a transformation. And every transformation deserves guidance.

By the third week, she could hold her baby without flinching. By the fifth, she was moving better, sleeping better, and—her words, not mine—dancing in the living room with her daughter again.

In her final session, she brought her baby along. The little girl babbled as Sneha smiled, a different woman from the one who first walked through our doors.

"You're not just a mom now," I said. "You're stronger than you were before."

She nodded, her eyes bright. "For the first time since delivery, I believe that."

The Outcome

Sneha didn't just reclaim her movement—she reclaimed herself. Her healing wasn't about chasing perfection. It was about learning to trust her body again, step by gentle step.

The Curve

Every new mother deserves to know: healing is possible, strength can return, and they are never broken—only becoming.

FORTY SEVEN

THE TAILOR WHO REFUSED TO BE STITCHED INTO PAIN

I first met Savita on a quiet afternoon. She arrived at The Flexion looking both out of place and quietly determined—a petite woman in her early fifties, her fingers stained with threads, her eyes heavy with exhaustion that went beyond the physical.

Savita wasn't just a tailor. She was the heart of her neighborhood—the one who stitched memories into fabric: wedding sarees, school uniforms, tiny dresses for first birthdays. Her hands had told stories for decades. But somewhere along the way, as she sewed life for others, her own life began to unravel.

"It started small," she told me, her voice barely above a whisper. "A tug in my lower back... then my neck, my hands... I thought it was just age."

She pushed through it, as women like her often do. Because deadlines don't wait. Because people count on you. Until one day, her son found her slumped over her sewing machine, silent tears slipping down her cheeks.

That's when she finally agreed to come in.

She sat stiffly at the edge of her chair, fidgeting with the hem of her dupatta. "Doctor... I'm not ready to give up my hands," she said softly. "Or my shop. That's all I have."

I met her gaze. "Then let's protect it," I said. "Let's protect you."

We began slowly. Breathwork. Tiny mobility drills. Movements that felt almost embarrassingly small at first. But the truth is, when your body has been locked into the same patterns for years— hunched shoulders, shallow breaths, rigid spines— these small shifts can be revolutionary.

"It feels silly," she said once, smiling shyly after a breathing session.

"It feels like change," I replied.

Week by week, Savita started noticing subtle victories. The ache between her shoulder blades softened. Her fingers steadied. She could sit longer without the burning pain that once defined her days.

Her world—once reduced to managing pain—began to expand again. She returned to her shop not just to work, but to live.

I still remember the day she carried a bundle of stitched clothes to a client—alone, without her son's help. She didn't announce it as a milestone. She simply smiled, her fingertips brushing the fabric she loved.

In her final session, she looked up and said, "I thought pain was just part of my price. But maybe... maybe I just forgot I could ask for more."

I smiled back. "Even the strongest threads need repair sometimes."

Savita left that day not just moving better, but living better. Her hands, her craft, her story—rethreaded, renewed.

The Outcome

Savita's journey wasn't about grand transformations. It was about remembering that healing isn't selfish—that every life, no matter how ordinary, deserves to feel whole.

The Curve

Pain tries to shrink us—our bodies, our worlds, our dreams. But sometimes, all it takes is a single stitch of belief to start sewing ourselves back together.

FORTY EIGHT

THE POTTER WHO MOVED BEYOND THE WHEEL

Ranga Rao had spent his entire life shaping clay. At sixty-five, he was one of the last traditional potters in his small village near Tenali, known not just for his craftsmanship but for the quiet dignity with which he carried a fading art form. His fingers knew the language of earth and water. His wheel spun not just clay but stories—of generations, of festivals, of gods and ancestors.

But when he arrived at The Flexion, he came not as a craftsman, but as a man bent by years of unseen burdens.

He walked slowly, his back hunched, his neck craned forward. The fingers that once molded perfect symmetry now trembled with strain. "The pain is not just in my back," he said softly in Telugu, "it has crept into my bones, my breath, even my prayers."

Ranga had tried everything his village offered. Herbal oils massaged by temple priests, turmeric poultices, prayers at the ancient Hanuman temple where he had offered earthen lamps every Saturday for years. "This is my karma," he said when I asked about the origin of his pain. "Maybe I angered some god by leaving work undone."

He had not seen a doctor before. For him, pain was part of life—something one bore silently, much like the cracked hands of a lifetime at the potter's wheel.

I examined him gently. His spine showed pronounced thoracic kyphosis with lumbar stiffness, likely from years of prolonged forward flexion, seated for hours at a time on a hard stone slab. His hip mobility was severely restricted, and his neck was locked into a forward posture. There were no signs of neurological compromise, but the mechanical strain on his joints, muscles, and soft tissues was profound.

He had accepted the story that age and karma were to blame. But I believed we could write him a new one.

We began slowly. The first sessions focused on breath—the very life force he had neglected in his fear of worsening pain. Seated diaphragmatic breathing calmed his hypervigilant nervous system. We added supported thoracic extension using a rolled towel—his first experience of opening the spine he had spent decades folding forward.

"The pot spins," he murmured once, "but I have forgotten how to spin myself upright."

We laughed together. Humor softened the edges of his deeply ingrained fear. I explained the science: how joints stiffen with immobility, how muscles weaken, how the nervous system can become trapped in patterns of protection long after danger has passed. He listened quietly but intently— absorbing each word like wet clay ready to be shaped.

As the weeks passed, we progressed to scapular retraction exercises, banded rows, and hip openers done in lying positions. Each movement was gentle but deliberate. He practiced at home on a mat near his small puja corner, lighting a diya before beginning as if to bless his own healing.

One day, I asked him why he hadn't sought help earlier. He smiled faintly. "In our village," he said, "we say that when the pot cracks, you don't blame the potter. You offer the broken pot to the river. I thought this pain was my river."

His words stayed with me. I reminded him that bodies, unlike clay pots, could reshape, could strengthen, could heal—even after years of wear.

We introduced functional training: squatting with support, half-kneeling positions, and loaded carries with small weights to build endurance. Each milestone he reached was met with quiet pride. His family noticed first—he no longer needed help standing. He began walking to the temple again, this time standing straighter.

I gently encouraged him to adjust his workspace—raising his potter's wheel slightly, changing sitting angles, alternating tasks. For someone so deeply tied to ritual and routine, this was hard. But slowly, he adapted.

One morning, he arrived with a small clay diya in his hand. "For you," he said simply. "Made it myself. No pain."

In our final sessions, Ranga Rao was a different man. His kyphosis wasn't completely gone—nor was it expected to be. But he moved with ease, he lifted with control, and most importantly, he returned to the heart of his craft with the knowledge that his body, like his clay, was still moldable.

He shared one last reflection: "I used to believe that some curses cannot be lifted. But now I see—it is not the gods who hold us down. It is the stories we tell ourselves."

The Curve

Sometimes healing is less about fixing what is broken and more about awakening what is still alive. In the space between superstition and science, between tradition and change, there lies the quiet power of movement—the reminder that even the most time-worn wheel can still turn.

FORTY NINE

THE TEACHER WHO STOOD HER GROUND AGAIN

Some people teach from textbooks. Others teach from the heart. Anuradha was the latter.

For over twenty-five years, she stood before dusty blackboards, animatedly bringing lessons to life—Shakespeare, algebra, history—her voice filled with energy, her hands forever in motion. She wasn't just a teacher. She was their teacher—the one who stayed after class, who showed up early, who poured herself into every student.

Until one day, her body simply refused.

It didn't happen dramatically. The pain crept in slowly: first a discomfort after long assemblies, then stiffness getting up from chairs, then a strange heaviness in her lower back. She brushed it off as "part of aging." Everyone gets sore, right?

Then, in the middle of a class, her right leg buckled. The chalk dropped from her hand. She barely caught herself on the desk. The room went silent—eyes of twenty children staring at her, confused, scared. That night, she wept—not because of the pain, but because she thought her story was over.

"I'm not ready to stop teaching," she whispered into the emptiness. "It's who I am."

That's how she found me.

Her first visit wasn't about scans or severity. It was about what mattered to her.

"What do you miss the most?" I asked.

Her eyes softened. "Standing without fear," she said. "Being able to give my best without feeling broken."

We started, as always, with gentleness. Awareness. Breath. Small movements that felt almost too simple. She had been standing for decades—but standing wrong. Knees locked. Spine stiff. Breath shallow.

Her spine, I explained, could relearn—just as she had taught so many students over the years.

Some days were discouraging. The pain flared. The doubts crept in. But something in Anuradha— something as steady as the chalk in her hand—held firm.

Step by step, her confidence returned. Not just in her body, but in herself.

She stood taller. Walked longer. Laughed louder. And one day, without realizing it, she stayed after class again—helping a student, explaining something with her usual warmth. Only later did she notice: she'd gone hours without thinking about the pain.

Her story wasn't over.

Her story was hers to write.

The Outcome

Anuradha learned she didn't have to choose between her body and her calling. She could carry both—differently, gently, and without fear. Her spine was never her weakness. It was simply her body asking for help.

The Curve

Some battles aren't about winning or losing— they're about remembering who you are, even when your body tries to make you forget.

And when you teach a teacher how to stand tall again, you don't just heal a back.

You help her keep shaping futures.

A Gentle Check-In

Every story in these pages carries one thread: movement—not just of the body, but of the heart and mind.

What's one small step you're ready to take to rewrite the story you've been telling yourself about your body or your life?

FIFTY

THE ELDERLY GENTLEMAN WHO CLIMBED ONE MORE HILL

For as long as I can remember, Mr. Iyer measured his life in footsteps.

A retired professor in his early seventies, he wasn't one to sit still. Mornings began with long walks through the park. Afternoons were for tending to his little balcony garden. Weekends meant short treks to the nearby hills—a ritual that reminded him he was still very much alive.

Until the hill won.

It happened quietly. A simple misstep. A sharp jab in the lower back. The familiar stiffness he'd occasionally felt over the years refused to loosen this time. His right leg grew weak. Climbing stairs became a struggle. His morning walks stopped. The balcony plants wilted.

Family members offered advice: "Rest." "Let it be." "You're not young anymore."

But that wasn't what unsettled him most. It wasn't just the pain—it was the shrinking of his world.

One evening, after weeks of frustration, his granddaughter handed him a printed brochure.

"Dadu," she said softly, "why don't you give this a try?"

The Flexion—Movement Beyond Pain.

Mr. Iyer raised an eyebrow. "At this age? What's the point?"

She smiled. "Because you still have hills to climb."

When he stepped into my clinic, I could see that familiar mix of skepticism and quiet hope. He looked around, slightly surprised to see people much younger than him.

I greeted him with a nod. "Mr. Iyer, what's the first thing you'd like to get back to?"

He didn't hesitate. "Walking. Without fear."

The first session was gentle. I noticed the guarded gait, the subtle hip stiffness, the shallow breathing—small things that add up to big limitations. But I also noticed something else: his spirit wasn't broken. Just buried.

We began slowly: weight shifts, breath work, small step-ups. He was skeptical. "This is too simple," he murmured.

I smiled. "Simple is where we begin. Freedom is where we end."

Week after week, something shifted.

Not just strength—confidence.

Not just mobility—freedom.

One day he caught himself climbing stairs without the banister. Another day he walked a full kilometer without a single pause.

And then came the day he didn't think would come again: he returned to his hill.

It wasn't the fastest climb. It wasn't the smoothest. But when he reached the familiar lookout point—his breath steady, his spine upright—I could see the quiet pride in his eyes.

In our final session, he said with a soft chuckle, "I thought growing old meant I had to slow down. I didn't realize I could just... keep going differently."

I nodded. "Movement doesn't retire."

He left The Flexion that day not as a man defined by years, but by motion.

The Outcome

Mr. Iyer reclaimed not just his movement but his independence. His pain no longer defined him—his willingness to move did.

The Curve

Sometimes the greatest climb isn't up a mountain—it's out of the beliefs that keep us still.

Age may slow the body, but the will to move? That's timeless.

The Doctor Who Had No Time to Heal

I've always believed the people who spend their lives taking care of others are often the last to take care of themselves.

Dr. Kiran was one of those people.

In his early fifties, Kiran was the kind of physician patients adored—steady, compassionate, always available. His life was a blur of hospital rounds, emergencies, night shifts, and endless giving.

But his own body had been quietly unraveling beneath the surface.

It began, as these things often do, with whispers: a stiff back after long hours on his feet, an ache after surgeries, a weariness he could never quite shake. He ignored it. There was always someone else who needed him more.

By the time he sat across from me, the polite smile he wore couldn't hide the deep exhaustion in his eyes.

"I know what I'd tell my own patients," he said softly. "But when it comes to me... I just don't have the time."

We started small: breath awareness, gentle mobility, pockets of mindful movement. But for Kiran, the real healing wasn't about the body—it was about permission. Permission to slow down. Permission to say no. Permission to tend to himself with the same kindness he extended to others.

Some days, he moved forward. Some days, life pulled him back.

The pain lessened but never fully left. His recovery remained unfinished—not because his body couldn't heal, but because his life rarely allowed the stillness it needed.

I still see him from time to time. Still working. Still giving. Still learning.

Some stories don't have neat endings. Some curves are still unfolding.

And sometimes, even those who heal must learn how to pause, breathe, and heal themselves.

FIFTY ONE

THE WOMAN WHO REFUSED TO BREAK

Geetha Reddy was thirty-four when the world quite literally forced her to her knees. A single moment—one misstep on a rainy day, one fall down a narrow stairway—and everything she thought she knew about her body shattered.

Her diagnosis: wedge compression fracture at L1.

When she arrived at The Flexion, she was not just broken in body but splintered in spirit. She walked in with the careful, fragile steps of someone who no longer trusted her own spine. Every breath seemed measured, every movement wrapped in layers of fear.

"I don't think I'll ever stand straight again," she said, her voice flat. "My life is finished."

I could see it—the terror beneath the surface. She had been told stories of lifelong disability, of permanent damage, of surgeries that might or might not work. Friends and family had filled her head with well-meaning but catastrophic visions. She was, in every way, caught between pain and panic.

Her scans confirmed the fracture: an L1 vertebral wedge with anterior height loss but no neurological deficit. Her neurosurgeon had rightly advised conservative management, but no one had prepared her for the emotional toll of that advice—the waiting, the helplessness, the fear that every small movement might worsen her injury.

We started, as we often do, not with movement but with reassurance. I explained the biomechanics of healing. I showed her the literature on how stable compression fractures without neurological involvement could and did heal well. I promised her that her spine, like her spirit, could rebuild.

The early sessions were slow. Supine diaphragmatic breathing. Isometric glute and quad contractions. Gentle hip mobility with no spinal loading. She flinched with every new position, her body bracing, her breath shallow.

"I feel like glass," she whispered once.

I reminded her: "Glass shatters. But you're more like clay—malleable, strong in ways you haven't rediscovered yet."

The drama of her emotions was real—every setback felt magnified, every ache interpreted as a sign of failure. She cried through some sessions, frustration boiling over. "Why me?" she asked more than once. "I wasn't doing anything wrong."

I let her speak. We cannot separate the body from the mind. Healing is never purely physical.

Week by week, we added movement: partial bridging, gentle supine knee rolls, resistance-free standing posture work. The fracture site began to stabilize. The pain eased in small increments—first in rest, then in motion.

We introduced pool therapy—an evidence-based approach for early movement without axial loading. She hesitated but then found freedom in the water. "I almost feel normal here," she smiled for the first time.

As her strength returned, so did her defiance. She wanted her life back—her independence, her dignity. We added light banded exercises, standing balance drills, core activation through supported movements. She pushed herself—not recklessly, but with purpose.

By the third month, she stood tall. Her posture no longer wilted under invisible weight. The scan at eight weeks confirmed good callus formation, stable alignment.

But it wasn't the scan that told me she had turned a corner. It was her eyes—alive again. Fierce.

In her final session, she said softly: "I thought this fracture had broken me. But it showed me who I really am. I'm not fragile. I'm unbreakable."

The Curve

Sometimes the spine bends. Sometimes it cracks. But the human spirit, when nurtured with patience, movement, and hope, can refuse to break. Healing is not the absence of scars—it is the courage to move despite them.

FIFTY TWO

THE COLONEL WHO SALUTED HIS SPINE ONE MORE TIME

Colonel Raghavan (Retd.) didn't believe in fuss.

He had served 28 years in the Army, led battalions across unforgiving terrains, and carried medals on his chest with quiet pride. Even after retirement, he woke before sunrise, folded his bedsheet with military precision, and performed his version of morning PT in the garden.

But age, as he discovered, doesn't salute discipline.

The pain crept in silently: stiffness after walks, a sharp jolt climbing stairs, a growing heaviness in his lower back that began to steal from him the small rituals that gave his life shape. The final straw came when his leg gave way on the stairs. Even the Colonel had to admit—something wasn't right.

An MRI showed disc degeneration and nerve compression. The advice was predictable: rest, painkillers, maybe surgery down the line. But he wasn't ready to surrender to any of it.

It was his son who convinced him to visit The Flexion. "They won't just treat the scan, Dad. They'll help you move again."

When I met him, he gave me a half-salute, half-smile. "Let's see if you can fix an old soldier," he joked.

I smiled back. "I don't fix, sir. I will help rebuild."

His assessment revealed what years of command had hidden: tight hips, a stiff thoracic spine, overworked lower back muscles. His body had compensated for so long it had forgotten how to move freely.

We started small: breathwork, gentle mobility, core activation. Movements that seemed almost too basic for a man used to marching in full gear. But they were exactly what his body needed.

Week after week, his posture improved. His steps steadied. The limping eased. He regained not just physical strength, but the quiet confidence that only movement brings.

By week seven, he was walking three kilometers every morning, standing tall without fear.

On his last day, he brought a photograph of himself leading a Republic Day parade. "This spine once carried the flag," he said softly. "Now it carries my groceries—and I'm grateful for both."

I placed the photo on the clinic shelf where it remains to this day.

The Outcome

Colonel Raghavan reclaimed his movement, his dignity, and his independence. He wasn't defined by pain. He was defined by resilience.

The Curve

Some battles aren't fought with weapons. They're fought with breath, patience, and the quiet courage to keep moving.

And sometimes, standing tall is the greatest salute of all.

FIFTY THREE

THE WOMAN WHO TOOK ONE STEP

Lalitha was 61 when she came to The Flexion, but the weight she carried made her look older—shoulders slumped, steps cautious, eyes tired. A retired school teacher, she had spent her life nurturing others, yet somewhere along the way, she had forgotten how to care for herself.

Her story wasn't new: chronic back pain that crept in silently, gradually stealing the small joys—morning walks, temple visits, playing with her grandson. Every movement became a negotiation between pain and perseverance.

Doctors told her what they often tell many: "It's just age-related changes. Manage it."

So she did—by moving less, fearing more, and shrinking her world.

When she first sat across from me, her voice was barely above a whisper. "I just want to be able to walk without fear," she said. "Not even far... just a little."

I nodded. "We'll start right there."

We began with breath—reconnecting her with a body she had long stopped trusting. Gentle spinal mobility, subtle core engagement, basic glute work. No grand promises. No timelines. Just one small step at a time.

Some sessions felt heavy. Some left her frustrated. But each time, she showed up.

By week three, she stood taller.

By week five, she could walk around her apartment complex without clutching her lower back.

By week eight, she returned to her morning temple visits—slowly, softly, but independently.

One day, she smiled through tears. "I never thought I'd feel normal again."

I smiled back. "Normal isn't gone. It just needed a new path."

The Outcome

Lalitha didn't just regain her mobility—she regained her dignity. Her story wasn't about conquering mountains—it was about reclaiming the simple freedoms that make life worth living.

The Curve

Some recoveries are quiet. They unfold not in leaps, but in tiny, consistent steps. And sometimes, one step—courageously taken—is enough to begin a new journey.

EPILOGUE

The Final Curve

Not every story ends with a cheer. Not every pain shows up on a scan. Not every recovery is neat.

But every story you've read in this book matters.

You've met people who were fractured—not always in bone, but in belief. Some rebuilt fully, others found peace in progress. Each journey is shaped by one unshakable truth: healing is not a destination. It's a direction.

Ramesh, the construction worker, still lifts loads—but now he listens to his body.

Arvind, the businessman, still wakes with stiffness—but he no longer wakes in fear.

Anita, the caregiver, still shows up for others—but finally shows up for herself too.

Mahesh, the farmer, still works the fields—but now with smarter, kinder movement.

They're not rare. They're not heroes.

They're people—just like you—navigating their own curve.

The Invisible Weight

Back pain doesn't scream for attention the way a cast does. It doesn't garner sympathy the way a visible wound might. It lingers quietly—stealing ease, sleep, and joy.

I've met people who looked perfectly fine but were fighting silent battles. I've seen tears behind confident eyes. Frustration behind smiles. Doubt behind strength.

And I've seen something else too:

The refusal to give up.

Even when progress is slow. Even when setbacks hit.

Even when the curve doesn't straighten—yet.

If You're Reading This in Pain

I may not know your story.

But I know this:

You are not broken.

You are not weak.

You are not too late.

Pain can drown out your identity. But it can change. And so can you.

I've seen people walk again when they thought they never would.

I've seen laughter return to faces that forgot what ease felt like.

I've seen scans lose their grip—and stories take their place.

Recovery isn't always pain-free.

But it can still be life-full.

The Stories That Stayed With Me

I still think of Ramesh—the pride in his voice when he said, "At least I can feed my family."

Of Arvind—who learned that money can't hurry healing.

Of Anita—who discovered that care doesn't have to come at her own expense.

Of Mahesh—whose strength was never in his back, but in his spirit.

These weren't grand breakthroughs. They were quiet ones:

The first deep breath.

The first night of uninterrupted sleep.

The first moment someone says, "Maybe I'm going to be okay."

Your Story Isn't Over

If you're here, you're still in motion.

You may be in the messy middle—the part that's murky and slow.

That's okay. Healing isn't about speed.

It's about staying. Showing up. Softening when you want to harden. Moving, even when you're unsure.

You don't need a perfect plan.

You just need a place to begin.

Start where you are.

Move a little. Breathe a little. Believe a little.

Ask for help. Rest when needed. Continue when you can.

Change is slow. But it is real.

And your curve—both spinal and personal—can still shift.

A FINAL INVITATION

Here's what I've learned after years of listening—not just to backs, but to the people behind them:

Movement is your ally.

Pain is not your identity.

And your story is not over.

Pain may pause you. But it doesn't define you.

Let this book be more than a read—let it be your reminder:

You're allowed to move.

You're allowed to recover.

You're allowed to return—to life, to hope, to yourself.

The final curve isn't just physical.

It's the shift in how we see ourselves:

Not as damaged.

But as capable.

Still unfolding.

Still healing.

Still moving forward—one steady, beautiful step at a time.

WHAT'S NEXT

Stronger Than Surgery

Releasing September 2025

If The Curve That Changed Everything made you rethink your back pain...

Stronger Than Surgery will show you why movement, not medicine, is often the first and best solution.

Built for both patients and physiotherapists, this next book digs deeper into:

How unnecessary spine surgeries happen—and how to prevent them

Why early physiotherapy matters more than ever

Real case examples, red/yellow flag decision-making, and clinical reasoning explained simply

It's a wake-up call for the over-medicalized spine—and a roadmap for those who believe in stronger, smarter care.

Releasing this September

www.ingramcontent.com/pod-product-compliance
Lightning Source LLC
Chambersburg PA
CBHW031947010726

47493CB00007B/2114